APPARITIONS ON THE ROCKS

A NOVEL

by Ryan Acker

*This novel is hereby dedicated to alcohol, the
most destructive narcotic ever formulated,
and the millions who enjoy it daily.*

Chapter One

W HEN I WAS a kid, I always saw gorgeous women riding shotgun in glossy European cars.

So when I made my first million, at twenty-three, the first thing I bought was a BMW Z4. It wasn't their most expensive model nor was it their fastest, but it was a really sexy little two-seater convertible with emissions that screamed: "This guy is worth fucking!" I drove it around Santa Monica and the South Bay, top down, well below the speed limit so that everyone could get a good look. It got me a lot of phone numbers.

When I was twenty-four, I decided to drive that Z4 up to San Francisco along the Pacific Coast Highway. It was supposed to be one hell of an experience, driving for eight hours alongside the ocean and through the rugged hills, the warm Cali wind blowing in your face. What could be better?

I'd received a bottle of thirty year old single malt scotch as a gift from my publisher and it rode shotgun, strapped in with the seatbelt to prevent it from spilling if I had to suddenly brake. The stuff was delicious, gentle and smooth as the skin of a woman's inner thigh, riddled with notes of chocolate, pear and honey to keep the palate fully engaged. I took back a shot every twenty minutes. It made for great company.

I'd left late in the day (I'd spent the previous night enjoying a bottle of agave tequila my agent had brought back for me from Guadalajara) so it was pitch black by the time I hit Big Sur. The road was two lanes wide, one in each direction and there were no street-lights, so you couldn't make out the ocean over the cliff's edge, let alone what was ten feet in front of you. I blasted the headlights. The bottle was already half empty.

I hadn't seen a car in over an hour and I was get-ting tired, so I started to increase my speed, little by little, 100 kilometers per hour to 110, 110 to 120, 120 to 140. The road was full of bends and turns through the mountains but the car handled as smoothly as the whiskey, 140 to 180, I was no longer driving, I was hang-gliding.

Still no cars, still no streetlights. Boredom set in. This route was fun only during the day. My vision was becoming blurry-I guess I was getting tired. Maybe I should pull over to the shoulder and sleep? Nah, someone might hit me, you can't see a goddamn thing on this road. Find a hotel? Maybe. How far did that last street sign say Monterey was? A good long swig of that delicious whiskey, 180 to 240.

And then, the car ran over something slick, I couldn't make it out but it felt like ice, even if it was California and it was July. The steering wheel locked and the car went into a drift, perpendicular to the road, hogging both lanes, sliding uncontrollably, making its way little by little out of my lane, through the oncoming one and over towards the shoulder: the edge of the cliff, who knew how far down to the ocean? My chest clamped and I stopped breathing as I pulled the emergency brake and fought furiously with the wheel to no avail, it wouldn't budge, I thought about jumping out, but at this speed the impact would tear my skin right off. Closer to the edge, only a few feet now, still moving fast, I could make out the waves below now, crashing against what looked like jagged rocks. I grabbed the bottle and took a massive swig, closing my eyes and preparing for the free-fall.

Only it didn't happen. The car stopped, on the shoulder, maybe a foot from the edge. I don't know how. I took a second to kiss the BMW emblem on the steering wheel. Thank God for German engineering.

I took a deep breath, another drink, and then drove the rest of the way to San Fran at half the speed limit.

CHAPTER TWO

FUCK SCIENCE. THE earth is flat.

We, all seven billion of us, will, with the bittersweet "joys" of age and experience come to know this all too well. When in our darkest hour, we find ourselves teetering, our tails between our legs, over the unforgiving edge, staring down with petrified pupils at the complete and total oblivion below.

And we can't claim ignorance. The message is nothing new. In five thousand years the game hasn't changed. Read Greek mythos and the warnings are crystal clear. We can put a man on the moon but that doesn't change the fact that we're shamelessly stupid, destined to make the same mistakes over and over again for all eternity. You can condition us, brainwash us, but nothing constructive you teach us will ever stick.

Too many great men and women have, on their deathbeds, used their last breaths to tell us how to be healthy, happy, how to prosper: smell, but don't taste the seductive, luscious fruit growing from trees who call out to us from shadowy corners. Seek warmth from, but, as you finally take flight, don't get too close to the soothing sun.

We understand what these warnings mean. Promises are made.

But then we do these things anyway, deriving plentiful pleasure in the process. Maybe it is in our very nature, to defy what's right, to work against our own self-interests, to ensure our own self-destruction. It is certainly in mine.

We all have our fruit, our sun, it takes many earthly forms. But regardless, when appreciation of this entity turns to dependency, you have only a short window before you're lost forever…

As someone whose soul is beyond salvage, I'd tell you to do things differently. But why bother? You won't listen anyway.

I never did.

* * *

The name on the book covers reads Sean O'Connor. The author's profile on their backs will tell you that I'm twenty-seven, that I'm Irish, first-generation Canadian, that I was bred and raised in Toronto, Ontario – the fifth largest city in North America (including Mexico). The profile will tell you that I currently reside in Los Angeles and that my books have sold pretty well. But there are a lot of things it won't tell you.

Some men are born with athletic prowess, others are graced with intellectual superiority, but with a father from the dirtiest pocket of North Dublin, I was granted neither. All I inherited from him was the thirst and it's non-negotiable. It's listed right after breathing on my personal variation of Maslow's hierarchy.

I laugh when I hear today's teenagers brag about giving away their liquid virginity at fourteen, as if that's supposed to be impressive. I had my first drink at eighteen months, some Irish cream my father poured into a sippy cup for me to enjoy behind my mother's back. He saw nothing wrong with it – his father had started him on whiskey at three weeks. "It's the best way to get the little bastards to stop crying," my grandfather used to say. To this day, drinking Irish cream triggers something innate in my subconscious, something incredibly reassuring – in the same way a baby blanket would for normal people.

Now that I've surpassed my physical peak, which most experts agree is twenty-six, I reminisce a lot more than I used to, about my childhood in particular. The memories range from bittersweet to nightmarish, but occasionally, I'm able to fixate on one that provides some pleasant nostalgia. For instance, I remember this one Saturday afternoon. I think I was seven, so it would have been 1991.

It was a sunny July day, starring a perfectly blue sky and a hint of crisp refreshing wind. My parents, my two older brothers and I all got up before the break of noon and eagerly made the trek together, by subway and bus, down to Woodbine Beach. There we had this entirely amiable picnic out on the sand, my mother's overcooked lasagna quite the sight for sore stomachs. I got a wicked sun-tan on my neck and back, as always I had refused to wear sunscreen, before we came to a consensus and shifted our post under this patch of blooming oak trees. When we had become too full to feast any further on the lasagna, some salad and a couple jugs of pop, we set aside the cooler and played touch football together along the boardwalk. Afterwards, to cool off, we jumped into the lake, without worry of its notorious pollutants, where we splashed around with a volleyball while my mother took photos to fill in the yearly album. On the way home, we found a gorgeous Black Lab sitting in an alley off Queen Street, abandoned, on account of a broken leg, so we took it home, where my mother mended it back to full health-before turning it over to a childless couple up the street. I like that memory a whole lot, even though it comes off sappy and childish-it reeks of a functioning family unit.

Come to think of it, there were a lot of great Saturdays. Playing soccer with my brothers in High Park, stuffing our faces with free fresh samples at the St. Lawrence Market, Jays games in the 500 bleachers, among many other nice outings. I guess, ultimately, things were pretty good during the day-my father was always too hung-over to do anything other than chug water and pop Aspirins like they were Tic Tacs as the nausea and migraines forced him to "play nice".

Everything's great-until the whiskey recedes below the paper label. At that point, those with good sense lock themselves behind solid doors, cover their ears and lie to themselves profusely until the screams, the thrashing-the complete and total chaos reduces itself to a quiet murmur.

Then the naïve take the bait.

By the time you're ten, you learn not to fall for

the comfort of initial silence-it's a trap, always is. Be patient, eyes closed. Be patient... You're hungry? Thirsty? Tired? Scared? Doesn't matter. Just keep hugging your bed, your dresser, your bathtub, any inanimate object will do-it'll make you feel better. They can't hug back, but they also can't hit you-a good trade in my eyes. Just be patient...

"It's not me, it's the bourbon. You know that. Don't you sport? That stuff, it's silly, that stuff it has a voice of its own, a life of its own. It takes me over, but it's not me. You know that, right? I love you and I'd never hurt you. You know that right? It's just the drinks. They're funny that way." My father would always say the morning after, substituting "bourbon" for whatever spirit he had consumed the evening before.

"Sure..." I'd always reply.

Initially you try to comprehend it, sympathize with it-it's your family after all, your blood. But then eventually you wake up one morning ripe with bruises, cuts and shattered bones and somewhere inside your head a switch is flicked, ridding you completely of that childish faith most kids take for granted. You grow up, way too fast.

Then you just learn to avoid it. You stay out late all the time, hit the empty gym at midnight, sleep on benches in the bum-ridden parks, a couch in a friend's basement, whatever. It's like waiting to catch a flight to nowhere. You bide a lot of time.

They all have a pass-out time, like clockwork. You memorize it for each night of the week and plan your arrival accordingly. They'll be mad that night when you don't pick up your phone, but whatever-they'll be too hung-over the next morning to care. Chances are they won't even remember-while they kneel in front of the toilet, their head entirely within the confines of the filthy bowl as they hack, cough and spit up 25 to 75 percent of the prior night's intake. The older they get, the greater the percentage.

They can't break that which they cannot contact, so sever all lines. Though, in the end, even with preparation, even with a good knowledge of the weather, you can't always miss the storm.

I'm thirteen, it's the winter of 1997, a quarter past midnight on a school night, it's one of the coldest days on record and it's too early, I really should wait another 90 minutes, but I'm freezing and have nowhere else to go. So I come in, lock the door behind me, take off my shoes oh so quietly, and then creep past the living room, where he's nestled and rowdy in front of sleazy TV infomercials with bikini models whose features improve with fatigue.

"Nice fucking tits, honey! Are you being a bad girl? Do you need some discipline?" he screams at the tube, and then he goes quiet, watching and listening intently, as if waiting for it to respond. When it doesn't, he tosses the bottle he's holding at the set. "Ah, you fucking stuck-up whore!"

I'm hungry, starving, I haven't eaten since lunch and puberty is kicking my hunger into overdrive, but to make a snack now would be far too risky, so I just head for my bedroom, one silent step after another, pinching my growling stomach to reduce the discomfort and the volume of the echoing grumbles. I wanna breathe, but it's too risky, so I hold it in and let my lungs ache for the greater good. Once I reach my room, I'll lock the door, push my dresser in the way for good measure and put on my headphones, blasting eighties metal to drown out the endless stream of threats he makes to my brothers and me and the vulgar sexual remarks he directs at my mum. Keep that music blasting, as high as my eardrums can tolerate, until the aftershocks finally evaporate. It'll be okay. Only a few more steps now, then I'm in the clear…It'll be okay… I'm standing directly in front of my door now, I reach out and take the handle…

He grabs me by the shoulder and tugs me back with so much force it tears my shirt. I turn and look him square in the eyes, the way he always demands.

"Hey! There you are! Where the fuck have you been! I've been trying to reach you all goddamn night!" He isn't a big man, he's only five foot nine, maybe 140 pounds, but he's cut, there isn't an ounce of fat on him and all his muscles sport an impressive definition, even though the only workout he ever gets is the bicep curl with a bottle. I'm already five-eleven and I hit the gym every day and yet I know I couldn't move him an inch if my life depended on it. The men in Ireland are so much harder than the ones here. Their bones are thicker, their pain tolerance limitless. Meanwhile, I'm tall and lanky, I grew way too fast: I trip over my own legs at least twice a day. Though I hate to admit it, I look a lot like him: we have the same light brown hair, the same dark grey eyes, the same toothy grin. My mum assured me that this was a good thing-he was quite the lady-killer in his prime.

"I've been out, just at the gym." I reply, calmly.

"Well, fuck! I have an emergency and I can't reach you, could you be any more fucking inconsiderate, for Christ's sake!"

"What's the emergency?" Crossing my fingers that my mother is okay, that he hasn't put her in the hospital again.

"I can't find the remote! You seen the remote? I gotta get up and walk ten

goddamn miles to change the fucking channel."

I let out a small breath of relief. "No sir, I have no idea." Keep those eyes glued.

"So where'd you hide it?" He asks.

"I didn't touch it."

"Then how'd you watch it tonight? Huh?" He's so full of conviction, so convinced that I'm out to get him. That everyone is. There's nothing I can say or do to persuade him otherwise. He's a bomb and I'm cutting the wires with no training, while the clock ticks down, one second after the other. Tick Tock.

"I didn't. I wasn't here tonight. And I haven't had time to watch it in weeks." I say, slowly, calmly, hitting every syllable so that there's no risk of him misunderstanding me.

He lets go of my shoulder.

"Really? So what? You saying that I'm a piece of shit? Huh? Cause I have time to watch it? That I have nothing better to do? That's what you're saying? That I'm a fucking loser?" He hits himself on the right temple, hard enough that the impact echoes. He hits himself a lot when he's drunk-the scars he sports are all self-inflicted.

And he is a loser – he dragged my pregnant mother

over here sixteen years ago, promising her a better life, but since then the prick hasn't been able to keep a job for more than a few months, always managing to screw things up just before the end of the probation period. My mum's the breadwinner, always has been.

After she'd prayed enough, with the rosary her mother had given her as a child, she would work up the courage to threaten to leave him if he didn't shape up. He would let her finish her rant and then, calmly, would assure her that if she ever left – he would find her and slit her throat. Knowing he was serious, she'd drop her head and go back to being the good little wife.

"No sir. You're not a loser." I can feel my heart begin to beat out of my chest, but I stay calm, keeping my right hand behind my back so he can't see it shake.

He strikes me across the face with the back of his hand while my mother and brothers watch silently from behind the banister upstairs. It's a common understanding: we all have to take turns. I catch their eyes and they give me a look, letting me know I can go to them when this is all over.

"You ungrateful little shit! I bust my fucking ass all day to clothe you! Feed you! And this is the treatment I get? I should bust your retard head in! You should have seen the way my old man dealt with this kind of disrespect! You think I'm hard? You have no fucking idea how we dealt with things back on the Isle. Fucking deadbeat kid! I ought to give you a taste." He clenches his fist – knuckles blistered and battered and grabs me by the collar.

"I'm sorry, sir."

"Sorry doesn't cut it! Find me the fucking remote,

now!" He lets go and shoves me down the hallway. "Get on it!"

I hustle into the living room and quickly check the top of the TV, the coffee table, the bookshelf, the obvious places, before he grabs me by the back of the head and throws me into the floor.

"Stay down there. Get a closer look." He spits onto the back of my head. For a few seconds I grit my teeth and tell myself that I'm stupid, that I'm weak, that I'm worthless shit.

I prop myself up onto my knees and search under the chairs, couch, fireplace, everywhere, while he takes swigs from a bottle of rye and laughs off sync at some seventies sitcom.

It's no use, the thing is nowhere to be found, but at least he's distracted, that buys me time to think. It's clearly not in here. Did he take it to the kitchen? The bathroom? The bedroom? There's a butcher's knife sitting in the kitchen sink, should I grab it and tell him I'll stab him if he hits me again? Will he buy the bluff? Or will he just grab it from me and use it to chop off a few of my fingers? I am debating this when a commercial break arrives. Time's up.

"So? Where is it, Sean!" He's ticking down, but I can no longer see the count.

I lock eyes with him again and sniffle hard to hold back some tears. "I don't… I don't know, sir".

"You don't fucking know?" He stands up again and removes his belt, revealing the remote, on his very chair. "What, are you fucking stupid, how could you not know?" He begins to wrap the leather around his fist.

"Sir. It's right there' I point to it.

"Huh?" He stops what he's doing and scratches his head.

"The remote. It's on your chair." I step forward and point to it again. "Right there, sir".

He looks down at it and laughs to himself. He hits himself across the face a couple of times. He smiles and groans after every blow. The pain really turns him on, gets him up.

He looks back to me and becomes utterly enraged.

"Who gives a damn about the remote? What, you want it or something? I'm watching the fucking TV, not you! This is my house! I pay the fucking bills!" The count is down to zero, you just hope the force of the initial blast knocks you out cold-so you don't have to feel the flames burning away your flesh. "I know…"

"You're crossing the line now, Sean!"

He shoves me into the carpet face first.

"Take it like a man, you little shit" he whispers before giving me twenty lashes against the back of the head with the buckle. It's made of iron.

And you can't move, you can't scream, you can't cry, it'll only make it worse – every sign of weakness brings with it another five strikes. So you learn to create a distraction, something to give you a place to hide within the confines of your mind while they explode on you for no reason

Mine has always been writing. While he hit me, I'd imagine being someone else, somewhere else, in a whole 'nother world. I'd create an alter ego and then an array of supporting characters, each with his or her own desires, conflicts and resolutions, people with problems far graver than my own. Then when I was free, I'd go to my notebook and scribble the ideas down. All of my early short stories were developed this way.

When he's done, I force myself back to my feet. I'm so numb that the pain is more or less gone, but my vision is blurry and my balance compromised. So I'm walking on a 45-degree angle, trying to get back to my room without falling over as I hug the wall for support, resisting the urge to vomit from the nausea and of course the even greater temptation to just completely break down.

"Hey! I'm not finished with you yet!" He hits me again, a backhand across the face. It isn't as hard as usual, but I'm so dizzy that I go down anyway.

"You don't seem to ever get it, Sean. I'm gonna have to give you something to help you remember." He picks up the bottle of rye and swigs back the remaining few ounces, then he smashes it against the brick fireplace mantle. Glass goes everywhere. A piece nicks his cheek, causing him to bleed, but he doesn't seem bothered. All that's left of the bottle is the stem and a few six inch shards. He grabs me by my hair with his left hand, holding it so firmly that if I pull away I'll be scalped for sure. Then, holding the bottle with his right, he drives one of the shards three inches into my shoulder. When he jerks his hand back, a piece of the glass breaks off inside me. I start to scream.

"Not so tough now, are you, smartass?" He puts a shard up against my throat, pressing it gently against my skin, any more force and it will pierce my jugular. "Shut your mouth or I'll push this right into your fucking neck." I press my front teeth into my lower lip, so hard that I can taste blood, but it keeps me quiet. That makes him smile, the same big smile I have-the one the women always tell me makes them blush. "That's my boy." He pulls the bottle away and lets go of my hair. "Now get the fuck out of my sight." He grabs a full bottle of vodka from under the coffee table and reassumes his position on the chair. He drinks forty or so ounces of liquor a night. Irish whiskeys are his favorite.

In the upstairs bathroom, my mother, a nurse, carefully removes the glass while my older brothers-Nick, one year my elder and Matt, three, assure me they'll kill him the next time he goes after them. My mother promises me that one day, everything will be okay. I hear these promises from them each and every time, but nothing ever changes.

* * *

When the blistering coil of the ruthless Canadian winters tore past my third-hand windbreaker and crudely knit Christmas sweater, right through my contemptuous soul, IT was but the one metaphorical match with the capacity to reignite the candle of my sanguinity, even if IT would flicker uncontrollably afterwards, under the demoralizing wind-chill, be that from rapidly fluctuating weather or the insult of lackluster minds.

I don't just wanna get warm... I wanna set myself on fire...

And in the dank summers, ones spent without the luxury of air-conditioning, IT was but the only mental wave with the ability to cool, to stop the drops-of sweat and tears, shed with equal frequency on those sweltering afternoons, hours utterly wasted, in suffo-cating captivity, within the confines of the East Toronto suburbs.

I don't just wanna dip my toes in, I wanna dive in head first…

And as I stood on the emotional railings of adoles-cence, one foot dangling recklessly over the merciless edge, IT was the gentle, reassuring voice, telling me to step back, to reconsider.

Not now…You've got Pulitzers to win…

And I listened…

And when I got my opportunity, I took it, without thought to the implications, to the consequences. I was young, things were simple.

I didn't bother to look back. My ticket to the "Promised Land" was a one way, in every sense of the expression.

Looking back, I have toppled every bridge with plentiful TNT, buried every advantage under six feet of solid concrete, nuked every emotional connection with an arsenal greater than that of the American and Soviet militaries combined, circa 1980. Looking back, there is no one to blame for all of this, but me. I have ensured my own demise. And in some perverted sense, I have enjoyed it.

This narrative, should be considered, what many alcoholics refer to as, "a moment of clarity"…

PART I

Summer 2011

Los Angeles, California

CHAPTER THREE

WHEN LOOKING AT a travel guide of L.A. you likely won't see a segment for Roxie's Tavern. A hole in the wall on a small side street off Abbot Kinney Blvd in Venice, right on the edge of Oakwood.

It was a depressing place, rundown, but not ironic enough to draw the hipsters from Silverlake. At one point it has been an upscale Irish pub. Now, the TV's no longer played football matches, just static, the darts were so dull they no longer stuck to the board and the Irish flag was stained with blood-the droplets of twenty or more men surrounding a long rip in its center which sooner or later was going to tear the whole thing in half. Amidst the restrained dampness of dried tears and the subtle smell of vomit, ever-worsening addiction was the steroid-infused elephant in the room. People didn't come here to laugh with friends-they came here to die alone.

Across Lincoln Blvd, things were better. Oakwood ended and the proceeding neighborhoods between there and the 405 were becoming overrun with the aspiring yuppies and creative wannabes priced out of Santa Monica and Marina Del Rey. The bars across Lincoln had a certain degree of self-respect. There, the blood and cum were tended to in a timely fashion.

To the north of the 10, things were far more civilized. Wealth and prestige demanded that the watering holes there be kept spotless, to hold bottles of chilled Cristal and Dom for the stars, the internationally celebrated "role models" who shat out thousands of their fans hard-earned dollars on their respective vices nightly and for the "actors", the clowns playing the part of someone competent enough to actually afford the bottle service-without falling even further into debt, in a once fabled economy now on the verge of complete disintegration.

Roxie's was not a place to find a woman for the mantelpiece or headboard. Though you could get a decent tug next door at the Korean parlor for $55.95 (or so I'm told). For most, Roxie's was the disgrace of the gentrifying neighborhood. For me, it was a chapel-for perverted communion. I came alone, for half-hearted forgiveness, four to five times a week.

"Hey *garcon*, another shot of bourbon, sans the rocks. Let's go! Chop Chop!" I ordered the tender with a clap of my hands.

He capped off the bottle and placed it back on the shelf.

"Hey buddy… I think you've had enough." He said. I had just watched him struggle with opening the cash register for an agonizing five minutes. He had all the dexterity of a gorilla, a gorilla with a learning disorder.

"Ah come on man, a couple more for a treasured

regular. What do you say?" I said, as suavely as I could after eight rounds.

"No. Sorry. Y'all are done. But I can give you some water if you want, or a soda?" He wore sleeves of meaningless tattoos, frustratingly cliché to the modern intellect, though the beach-bum brunettes probably found them sexy. His hands still reeked of his latest "conquests". He was a guy who would never need to buy deodorant-he wore a different woman's perfume every day. This reality was utterly tragic. Before the invention of steroids this idiot would have died a virgin and rightfully so.

I pulled out my wallet. "Alright, name your price."

"What?"

"For the next drink. How much?" I asked him.

"I can't give you anymore. I'm sorry."

"Twenty? Fifty? A hundred? What? You think I care? Do you have any idea who I am?" Maybe he didn't, the bozo was probably illiterate.

"Yeah, I know who you are but you're not getting anymore. I think I'm gonna need to ask you to cash out."

It was so close and yet so far. My palate was an arid desert, parched and cracking along its fault lines, it needed to be hydrated post-haste and I didn't have time to start a tab elsewhere. So I reached across the bar and grabbed him firmly by his collar. "Listen to me, you dumbass meathead. Give me another drink, now!" He was a huge guy and despite having gained three inches since I was thirteen-I was still pretty lanky. But I wasn't the least bit afraid of him-his bicep looked so fake I figured the prick of a pin would completely deflate it.

The door to the bar swung open and Carlos, the manager entered, along with two older women with gigantic asses and the stench of cigarettes baked into their skin. I let go of the tender and Carlos gave me a smile and a wave. He liked having a celebrity to "class up" the joint.

"Carlos! This guy has to go! He's totally out of line!" The tender said of me. "The psycho just grabbed me!"

I expected Carlos to stand up for me, considering the amount of cash I dropped in his shithole each and every week it was the least he could do. Maybe he'd even give me a round on the house. "Okay, so cash him out! Deal with it!" Carlos replied casually, he was in a frantic rush to get these women into his office and pull down the window curtain.

"Tough shit, pal," the tender said to me with a cocky smirk. "Now pay your tab and get the hell out of here. Touch me again and famous or not, I'll bury your ass, you're a long way from Beverley Hills, bitch."

As soon as he turned his back, to prepare my bill, I jumped over the bar and grabbed the Texas mickey of bourbon under the time-honored mantra of if you want something done right, just do it yourself. Though apparently, in the Venice Beach dive-bar scene, self-serving is considered a bit of a "no-no". Even Carlos agreed with that, with some accompanying kicks to my ribcage while the bouncer held me down so the bar-tender could throw me a beating in the bar's rear storage room. After they were satisfied, they announced my 86. When I was out of their sight, I pulled out my phone and added it to the list.

CHAPTER FOUR

A ND THAT'S WHY I turned up to the 2011 American Writers' Expo at LAX-for which I was the guest of honor, looking like a washed-up boxer who had gone down cold in the first. Far more sober than I should have been, than I needed to be, to tolerate their constant badgering. Nowadays every schmuck with an internet connection and a blog about his cat is a literary critic.

"Ladies and gentlemen. I'm proud – no, honored, truly, to present-the guest of honor at this years AWE. He's a best-selling author with three successful works under his belt. He's Canadian-born though now residing here in lovely Los Angeles. Please give a warm welcome to Mr. Sean O'Connor!" The MC announced with a tremendous fervor.

Unanimous applause. The occasional whistle. I gotta admit, it got me a bit hard. Always did. So I wore a smile as I took the stage, grabbed the mic from the MC and stared off into the enormous crowd, sitting thirty rows deep on cheap fold-out chairs, their eyes, their complete attention, focused on my mouth. Every time

I made eye contact, they looked away nervously, they were all so intimidated. It made me feel really special.

There was nothing I enjoyed more than talking about my writing or about the mechanics of the industry with like-minded individuals, but that wasn't why I was here. These people didn't come here for a dose of reality-of course not. They braved the rush hour drive and three-figure ticket because they wanted their own nurturing bubbles of fantasy further inflated – the fundamental of any profitable seminar.

So I swallowed my pride and, with all the honesty of a politician a week away from election, gave them the usual bullshit spiel, quarter-heartedly at best, the routine ten-minute stock speech about how if they "give it their all" and "chase the dream" they too can make it in the exciting world of fiction, the kind of jargon that I, as a naive, underprivileged kid, had also believed to be true. Then, only because I was contractually obligated to do so, I opened it up to questions, what was left of the tranquillizer rapidly wearing off.

"Mr. O'Connor? I'm sure you get this question every day, but when is *Ten Feet Down* going to hit shelves?" She was short, blond and studious, her accent hinting that she was an East Coast girl, her erratic, rutted teeth that she was from a poor family, the brand new IPhone she was filming the session with, that she was now with something to prove. She had made the trek west as part of some poetic process of self-transformation. She'd do her undergrad out here, in English or Journalism. And then, unable to find work in an age of credential inflation, would return back east, in debt and utterly disenfranchised. Oh if she only knew… *Ten*

Feet Down was my current work in progress, my long-awaited fourth novel, but I hadn't written a fresh sentence of it in over two years.

"What's your name, sweetheart?" I asked her, my tone fun and flirty.

"Beth. And I'd appreciate it if you didn't call me sweetheart, Mr. O'Connor." She kept a straight face and a cold tone – boy, was she uptight, from a religious family, no doubt. There was no sense in being charming. My chances at bedding her after the conference were 10 percent, at best.

"All apologies, Beth. You know I actually do get that question everyday, so thanks for being the millionth person to remind me of my own incompetence."

"Well. I think your readers have the right to know."

"Fair enough. Hey. I love you guys-I'd be back in Canada serving up poutines without you. But, see, I'm suffering a near fatal instance of what most of you would call writer's block. I'm about three-quarters of the way through; I just can't seem to put together a good ending. But if you give me your number, sweetheart, I'll personally keep you posted." Maybe I could, however sleazily, make her at least crack a smile.

"No thanks." No dice.

She sat down, embarrassed and unsatisfied and another vulture promptly took her place: a nerdy know-it-all, a pretentious, old-money, over-educated prick, ripe with a sweater vest and frameless glasses, multiple degrees "earned" though ultimately pointless; he would never need to work a real day in his life anyhow. He collected doctorates at Ivy League institutions like they were matchbooks.

"Mr. O'Connor" He spoke with a British accent, but he was clearly American.

"Please, call me Sean."

"Well, Sean. Don't you think three years is a little long for a single novel?" The way he said it felt more like a cross-examination than a question.

"What's your name, kid?" I asked him. Even though he was a few years older than me.

"Brinkley. Jonathon Brinkley."

"Tell me, Jonathon Brinkley. How long does it typically take *you* to write a polished 60,000 word novel?"

He didn't hesitate. "My last one? About six months."

"Really?" Six months? Wow, it used to take me six months to finish a rough draft.

"Yes. The one before that, four." He replied. "And that was while working on my second Ph.D." He added as he adopted this big smile and watched me intently. I guess he figured he had me trapped. The rest of the crowd stared at me too, awaiting my comeback. I didn't have to think long, I'd been in L.A. for quite some time, I knew how to shatter confidence. It was as natural as breathing.

"Well. Mr. Brinkley, how many copies have you sold of each?"

"Sold?" The word appeared foreign to him.

"That's still what we do with books, isn't it? So come on. How many? A million? A hundred thousand? What?"

"I'm still in the process of agent hunting…" That was what I thought. Six months my ass.

"So you haven't sold even one lonely copy. Not even to your own mother?"

He broke eye contact with me and reestablished it with the floor. "Not yet, no. But," *What a waste of my time.*

"So really, you don't know what the hell you're talking about. Next!"

Yet another overly inquisitive mind. This one older, in his forties or fifties, conservatively dressed in a three-piece brown suit. An English professor, I figured. Meaning he was rich in theory but desolate in the practicality that, in this business, was all that really mattered. How you could teach writing without having written a book yourself was well beyond me.

"Sean?"

"Yep?"

"I was hoping to get your two cents on the film adaptation of *Anything for a Dollar*. My students are doing a report on it for their final ISU." Ah, the bane of my existence: the latest movie and, without question, the worst one yet. I had walked out of the premiere around the forty-five minute mark.

"Your name?"

"Willard. Willard White. Professor Willard White." He must have thought it would impress me. It didn't.

"Well, Will. I thought it was a piece of shit. I never imagined my precious dark little gem of a novel about an inner city crack whore would be turned into a light hearted feel-good romcom with teeny-bopper actors and a happy ending, but hey, Hollywood never fails to disappoint, now does it? Next!"

"Do you have any advice for young writers? I'm

Neil, by the way." Neil wore Gucci sunglasses and a Rolex Daytona watch, but he lacked the accompanying social equity. He probably told the girls in Hollywood he was a self-made millionaire, or maybe the only child of an old money family, but in the end, he was just another spoiled kid-living the dream off his upper-middle-class parents' battered backs.

"Sure, Neil! Find another profession. It means less competition for me. The last thing L.A. needs is another starving writer. Next! Let's say one more."

She was a beautiful girl, in a classical sense: dressed down, face void of makeup, her demeanor subtle and unassuming, unintimidated by me and my successes. I could tell she was here not to list off another cliché question, but to attempt to properly challenge me. I gave her my full attention. "Mr. O'Connor. I know I won't be the first to ask, but I really want to know. In all your books you always have one unnamed female character, where you capitalize every reference to her, you know? SHE, HER, et cetera, What's the deal? Who's the girl, the one that got away?"

She wasn't the first to ask, and I wasn't going to let her be the first to get the answer.

"That's all the time I have." I said. "Thanks, everyone, for coming out. Be sure to visit my website for updates and merchandise." I didn't wait for the MC to return, I just dropped the mic to the stage and stormed out. It was my fault, really, I should have come more prepared, I should have had more to drink…*much* more…

CHAPTER FIVE

"THE HELL WAS that, Sean?" screamed Mark Hanson my agent and friend of five years. "What did we discuss, huh! You promised me you were going to act professionally up there! Take questions from the fans seriously! That there would be no more bullshit antics!" We sat across from one another in an over-priced airport bar for a debrief he insisted we hold after every public event. Mark was a good-looking guy: stylish, athletic, shiny ocean blue eyes, constant tan, but he was way too young to have as many grey hairs as he did. He was aging like a president and I was his Iraq.

"Relax, Mark." I said. "They love it-the potty mouth, being talked down to. They eat that stuff up. It's all part of the persona, the brand." I wasn't writing children's fiction, transgressive authors were supposed to be assholes, I assured myself, while taking back a long sip of an oatmeal stout.

"You've been drinking again, haven't you?"

"No. I."

He cut me right off. "Bullshit! I can smell it on your

breath." He leaned forward and took a good whiff. "The scotch!"

"Bourbon, actually." I corrected him.

"Christ, Sean! You told me you had it under control. You swore to me!"

I bit my lip, broke eye contact and ran my hands through my hair. "I'm sorry, all right? It's not what you think! I started drinking again because I couldn't write, not the other way around."

He sighed and rubbed his temples, which exaggerated the deeply entrenched stress marks on his forehead. "Well, it's not helping things, now is it! First we promised them 2008, then 2009, then 2010. I can't keep putting this off! Sooner or later they're just gonna tell us to piss off! Yes, you used to be a pretty big deal, but there's a million younger, better writers anxious to take your place, Sean! Don't ever forget that!"

"This year, Mark. I promise. I'm only 15,000 words away. I'm doing this right, so it's gonna push a million when it's done. Keep you safe and secure in that new Laurel Canyon castle with the old ball and chain." I gave him the O'Connor trademark smile, hoping it might charm him into calming down and buying me another round.

He raised his fist as if he were going to strike me but let it flail ruthlessly against the wall instead, leaving an indent. He might have been only thirty-nine, but everyone in the industry knew, he lived by the old-school Hollywood mindset. But I liked that. When you're a writer you want the scariest son of a bitch you can find in your corner. My dad would have made a great agent.

He grabbed my wrist and began to squeeze it. "Listen. I'm gonna tell you two things, Sean. The first as your friend, the second as your agent, okay? First, you gotta cut out this crash-course bullshit, okay? You're drinking yourself half to death, and for what? We've sold five million copies together-five million! Enough to put your name on bestseller lists from L.A. to Tokyo. You're living in a gorgeous penthouse downtown and you've got the love of a beautiful woman who for some reason completely beyond me – stands by you through thick and thin. What could be so bad? Huh? What?"

"Mark."

He slammed my wrist onto the table hard enough to leave a bruise. "Shut up! Second. I can't keep spending all my time bailing you out. Believe it or not, but I've got other clients, other responsibilities than just you. So here it is. If *Ten Feet Down* isn't on my desk, ready for editing by Christmas, you and I are done professionally, you understand?"

"Come on you don't mean that…" He was a persistent son of a bitch who never gave up on anything worthwhile.

He let go of my wrist and began to prod his finger into my face. "I do, Sean, I really do. So put down the Goddamn bottle, dry up, get behind your laptop and punch out what's left of this sucker, okay? You can do this. You've jerked around long enough. Had your fun. Now, it's time to produce."

"I'll do my best." I brought the pint glass back to my lips only to have him knock it away from my face, onto the floor. The entire glass spilled. That really bothered me – good beer should never go to waste.

"This is Los Angeles, Sean." He said. "Out here, that's just loser talk. You wanna get by on just "your best" go back to Canada and write for the BCB."

"You mean the CBC?"

"Do I look like I give a shit?" He did not.

He finished his pint in one long gulp, dropped a hundred to cover the twenty – five-dollar bill and the wall damage and stormed out. I'd gotten him mad before, but nothing like this.

I would start writing tomorrow, I promised myself.

* * *

I didn't feel inclined for another dive bar beating, so I pulled a one-eighty and classed things up. I drove my newest toy, the BMW 750I, to the glossy, star-riddled Sunset Strip, where I opened a tab on my no-limit platinum at a posh little lounge called Mothership. It played house music at a reasonable volume to convert bar banter into respectable conversation and it was bright enough in there to actually make out faces. Every one of them was well dressed, organized into different clichés: the businessmen with their single malt, the socialites with their martinis and the D list actors with their bottles of faux champagne, they were spread out across a few couches, booths, love seats and the central bar, where I took my position right across from the tender.

"Hey, gorgeous! Looking sharp! What can I get you?" She was a local, a real Valley Girl: plain, poor, honest and blunt, so I took it as a genuine compliment.

"Well, I've got my own drink. It's two shots of bourbon mixed with two of tequila." I said. "Can you just keep those coming until last call?"

"A man who knows what he wants. Sure honey." She gave an exaggerated wink.

There was a faint tap on my shoulder-the woman sitting next to me. "Excuse me" She said. I'm sorry to bother you. I don't normally do this, but are you Sean O'Connor?" She was tall, blond and infused with silicon, "fuck me": printed in bold invisible ink right on her accentuated bust.

"And what if I am?" I replied playfully.

"Oh my God!" She rubbed my arm affectionately. "You're totally my favorite writer! Like, you're so good! I like can't even believe I'm sitting next to you right now!"

"Thank you. Always nice to meet a fan." Well, when they were this attractive.

"Oh my God, am I ever! I've like read all your books, two times each."

"Wow. That's two more times than me."

She paused, then laughed. "Oh I get it! And who knew you were funny too?"

"I'm just full of surprises." I gave her a wink while taking a sip.

"I'm Kristy." She moved her hand from my arm down to my chest.

"Nice to meet you, Kristy." I took her hand and kissed it gently. "*Enchantè* "

"What? Oh that's French, right?"

"Yeah." It was one of the ten words I still remembered from high school.

"Right! I totally forgot you were Canadian!"

"Bred and raised."

"Really? Are you sure? I haven't heard you say *eh* once." Oh boy.

"So." I said. "What do you do, Kristy?"

"I'm, well, I'm an actress." She pressed her palm to her breast.

"Oh, really?" In adult productions?

"Well. I will be. That's why I came to L.A. I used to do some modeling back home. Denver, that's where I'm from. And everyone was always like, Kristy, you should totally go to Hollywood and become a famous actress and I was like, yeah! That sounds so perfect! So I quit my job and grabbed the first bus. I have my first big audition next week."

"Oh yeah? Right on." My interest was starting to wane, but another glance at her chest restored it.

"Yeah, I mean, it's a small part, only like two lines, but it's a prime-time soap. And you know how those are-once you get on, you have work till you're dead."

What she lacked in intellect she more than made up for in youthful enthusiasm and potential sexual maneuverability. Hell, the things I could do to her...I thought of a few more elaborate scenarios and felt myself get hard.

"So, Kristy." I said. "What do you say I buy you a drink? Some Pinot? Shiraz? Cabernet maybe? " I grabbed the nearby wine menu and began to browse it for something from Napa.

She gave me a dumb clueless gaze. It was her calling card-I guess some men would find it endearing. "Some what?" She asked.

I put the menu down. "Or some Champagne, perhaps?" No woman in the history of ever has said no to that.

"Um, I'd totally love some, but I don't know what my boyfriend would think of that." Ah no, the "B word", the ultimate buzz kill. The blood began to flow back to my brain.

"Boyfriend?"

"Yeah! He's coming in for the weekend from Colorado. I'm meeting him here tonight, actually." Dammit! I turned back to my drink.

She put her hand down onto my knee and then slowly moved it up to my groin, where she left it resting. "But, I could totally use some company until he gets here." She said, as she began to massage me and I heard myself let off a satisfactory groan.

I told the tender to watch my drink.

She gripped my hand and led me to the back of the bar, to the bathrooms. All of them were private. Inside the countertops were marble, the toilet self-cleaning and the scent of fresh jasmine filled the air. I locked the door.

I moved in to kiss her, but she turned her head away so all I caught was her cheek.

"What?" I asked.

"That's not what I want." She replied with a giggle.

She pulled down my pants and proceeded to give me a stellar blowjob with all the fixings while I ran my hand over her firm fake breasts. Midway through the performance I rolled my right hand up her dress, questing for her panties. She stopped what she was doing and slapped my hand away. "Nuh-uh!" She said.

"What? Why not?" I asked her, as I proceeded to run my hand up her leg once more. "Sharing is caring." I added.

"It's my lame time of the month." She replied, and I promptly retracted my hand.

She finished, we tidied up and returned to our seats. She kept talking, I stopped listening.

About ten minutes later, a guy entered the bar, twenty-five, unshaven, hair below his ears, dressed in a plain white t-shirt and baggy jeans, he waved to Kristy and she ran into his arms. I promptly moved to a chair further down the bar.

The two of them chatted about worthless nothings for a few minutes and then he headed for the washroom. Kristy turned her attention back to me.

"So. I've gotta get going." She said. "But it was so nice to meet you, Sean O'Connor!" We had a quick hug-I loved the feeling of her breasts against my chest.

"Likewise, Kristy."

"I can't wait to read *Ten Feet Down*. In the meantime, I have something you can read…" She said, handing me a folded-up napkin: *He's only in town a few days, same with Aunt Flo, call me Monday and we can do some heavy "reading" 555 668 5868*

A writer being treated like a rock star – only in L.A.

* * *

Over the next two hours, deprived of further company, I whipped back five of my drinks and then just indulged in the tranquility of it all. The fact that I could postpone my responsibilities, my obligations, one last time and just live in this moment, this black box which kept me dry from all the prevailing storms of harsh, calculating reality. And I laughed, laughed at nothing, and I flirted, flirted with no one and I smiled, smiled at nothing even remotely happy, myself, none the wiser, until dreaded last call. Which, in L.A, always came two hours too soon.

* * *

The lights came on, the music stopped and the place began to empty out in twos or fours.

"Hun, I hope you're not planning on driving" the Valley Girl proclaimed.

"Why not?"

"Please, you just drank half my bar, give me your keys." She stuck out her hand.

"What?" When did this become a public service announcement from MADD?

"I gotta take 'em. Bar policy. That or I have to report you to the police. You can come by and pick 'em up tomorrow."

I reached into my silk pockets and dropped the keys onto the polished counter.

"So." I said. "You offering me a ride? I actually can't remember my address-maybe you could give me yours instead?" It was a stupid line but I'd always wanted to use it.

She chuckled and held up her left hand, a subtle white ribbon of truth on her ring finger. "I would, I really would, if I wasn't taken, sweetie. I got a real thing for a man who can spell properly."

"I'm flattered."

"Though-I'm just aching, begging, dripping wet, for a nice big, tip." She tapped on the bill.

"Fair enough." I chuckled.

"Which means I need to make sure you get home safe. Want me to call you a cab?"

"No, it's okay. I'll just take the subway."

She looked down at her watch. "At Highland? Sweetie it's already 1:35. Let me get you that cab, okay?" God, at times like these, did I ever miss the "Vomit Comet." The late night bus, running up Yonge, Toronto's Main Street, crowded refuge for stranded inebriated souls, be they lost or accompanied, those souls who were too busy enjoying themselves or wallowing in misery to leave in time for the final subway. And it wasn't that L.A. didn't have night buses-it did, I could have taken the #4 and been home in an hour, but in L.A., "normal" people didn't use buses after dark, especially after midnight.

"No it's alright. I hate cabs." I replied.

"Well, is there someone who can pick you up?" she asked.

I didn't want to wake her. Unlike me, she had to work in the morning. Nor did I want to test Mark's patience any further – or worse, let him know I was soaking wet. "No. I'll just walk, it's ok." I said.

She laughed. "Walking in WeHo? Do you live nearby?"

"Yeah, I'm right on Sunset." I had to lie. She never would have believed I intended to walk across nearly the entire city, a two-and-a – half hour journey if I hustled. I could hardly believe it myself, and yet I was a bit excited at the prospect, it would be an adventure. There were far too few of those, these days.

"Happy to hear that!"

Her attitude was understandable though still a little disheartening. She came off as if she was really concerned, actually invested in my well-being, though behind the mid-sized, partially exposed breasts and frequent semi-charmed smiles, it was only because she was sure of a generous gratuity from the only genuine millionaire in the room. Bartenders-what an effective metaphor for the moralistic bankruptcy of our consumerist culture.

"Okay. Well have a nice walk. It will do some good to sober you up."

In disoriented inebriation I tipped her 100 percent of the ludicrous bill, left my car locked and as secure as could be in a back-alley parking lot off Fountain Ave and began the pilgrimage eastbound toward Flower Street and the 4,000 square-foot penthouse overlooking the Staples Center, that I called my home.

When I first bought it, leaving my Redondo Beach two-bedroom behind, most people labeled me certifiably insane. After all, here in the land of the automobile, no one with an option chose Downtown, an eastside neighborhood that no one save those on social assistance, considered central to anything worthwhile. "West of Fairfax or north of Beverly", or your lease was a death sentence-well, that's what the snotty self-proclaimed experts said anyway.

But, I liked it-far preferred it to the ostentatious drivel of the west-side. I was forever a city boy, and it was the only part of town that felt distinctly urban.

And-at the very least, when I was messed up enough, I could very easily confuse its skyline for that of Toronto's King Street.

I will admit, I was surprised – amazed really-that I was able to make it all the way to Westlake before running into a confrontation. Heading south on Fairfax and then east on 6th, I saw-maybe two other normal people out and about on foot. The rest were on the street because they lived there, but they didn't give me any real problems. One guy followed me for a few blocks through Mid-Wilshire-until I gave him a quarter to stop, whatever-no big deal.

But here I was in Westlake, the neighborhood just west of the 110 and my world in Downtown. It was known primarily for two things: 1. MacArthur Park: a cesspool serving as a market for drugs, weapons and fake IDs. 2. Some pretty stellar Central American cuisine. It was one of about thirty areas Mark had advised me never to enter. So if I wanted to eat, I got delivery.

I tensed up as soon as I saw them. Three kids, probably no more than fifteen or sixteen years old. They weren't looking for anything in particular as they sat around the fringes of the park at 3:30 a.m., sharing a pipe of rock, fiddling around with a rusty butterfly knife. They didn't intend on causing trouble: their only real agenda was to get inebriated and laid (which, to be fair, is generally mine as well), but it didn't help that I was dressed in a six-thousand-dollar Armani suit-the one Mark insisted made me look more reliable in the eyes of the publishers – and fiddling for gonzo porn on a brand-new iPhone.

It had been way too long since I'd last walked

anywhere farther than the ever more strenuous ten feet from the gated parking lot to my condo's guarded entrance. And it had been years since I'd last walked a step between the Fig and the 405. In Central L.A., the long since abandoned core, to be successful was to push your luck. But when I was drunk, my inner judgment still lived in Canada, where you could walk alone day or night, nearly anywhere and not fear for your safety. Oh, those were the days.

"Hey, fairskin. You got the time?" In L.A., there is no correct answer to that question.

"Nah, man, sorry." I said and kept walking, my gaze on the horizon. Eye contact can be misconstrued as a threat.

"Yo. How bout a light?" This answer must be even more carefully constructed.

"Sorry, guys, don't smoke." I caught a look at them in my peripheral vision. They weren't budging. Another ten feet and I'd be in the clear, like I always had been when crossing through Moss Park, Toronto's version of Skid Row, to see an old flame over in Leslieville.

But, no, this wasn't Toronto and the largest signaled to the other two that I was a worthwhile mark. I didn't wait for them to get up before I sprinted full out, toward the glistening Downtown Westside skyscrapers that promised safety, the end of gangland and the return of respectable civilization, just a mile away.

"You're ours, puto!" they shouted after me.

I had ten years on them, but I was still faster, sprier, as I flew down 6th street. I gained on them with each passing block, my allies the office towers pulling me in like a magnet. I was convinced I was going to make it until the twenty or so ounces finally caught up to me and I plunged, clumsily, face first onto the cool concrete.

Warning: When you're utterly hammered, objects in rear may be closer than they appear.

"Not so fast are ya? Fuckin' suit! You're up in the wrong hood motherfucker!" He drove his skater shoe into the side of my flustered head, the blow harsh enough to disorient my cranium slightly more than my adult-flavored medicine.

"You think yous in Brentwood? This is Westlake, bitch! You're gonna have to pay a toll! So let's see you empty those pretty little pockets!"

I tossed over the phone, the keys and the wallet, too hammered to consider the implications, too tired for further conflict.

They rustled through the bare snake-skin wallet, its cash having been converted to ounces hours ago.

"Uh oh…Where's the green, man?"

I let out a deep desperate breath. "That's all I got-take the phone, it's top of the line, sold out all over the city."

He inspected it for a second and then smashed it against the cement, shattering the screen.

"You think I want a phone? I got a fucking phone! I want some cash. Now!"

"The phone was worth a lot of it."

He pressed the knife up against my throat. "You think you're funny, don't you, white boy? You think 'cause you rich you won't get none? You better get me some money right fucking now, or I'm gonna take the toll out in flesh, ya feel me?"

I took them to the nearest ATM, an outdoor one at a gas station across the street that had already closed for the night and withdrew the machine's allowance- two grand.

"Yeah! That's what I'm talking about, baby!" one of the kids shouted, anxiously bouncing from side to side every time another fifty evacuated the machine.

So tired. I just wanted to hop into bed next to her and drift off, but the guys didn't seem in any rush to run away with their new-found fortune. I figured I'd try and appeal to reason. "Look guys." I said. "I've got a killer headache, you've got your money, we're done here."

They looked at each other as if silently negotiating where to go from there. "Nah man." Said the biggest kid. "I say we just getting started. Your house, take us there. Rich bitch like you probably got a safe."

"I don't have a"

My second black eye in twenty-four hours. This one hurt even more.

"I wasn't *asking* you, motherfucker! Take us there, now!"

Risking myself was one thing. When I was wasted I didn't give a shit. But even in this state, I couldn't even consider putting her, Stephanie, in harm's way.

"No." I had a good seven inches on their largest guy, so I pressed myself up into him. "We're finished."

"Who the fuck you think you're talking to? Huh?" He pressed the knife into my stomach. "We're going or I'm gonna fucking carve you up! Motherfucker walks right into my hood like he owns the place, you're gonna be taught a real lesson tonight!"

I'm Irish, fighting is in my DNA. My bones were now as thick as my father's and my skin had become leather armor. I could have been a boxer if not for the fact that I only ever fought when I had something to lose. But when I fought, I fought to win. "Fine!" I told him. "We'll do it your way!"

I grabbed his wrist a few inches north of the blade and snapped it in one quick motion, then drove him to the ground with my desensitized forehead. For good measure, I gave him a roundhouse kick to his temple. That one put him to sleep.

Another kid charged me unarmed and I put the prick down with one brash back – hand to his brittle, malnourished jaw. I heard it crack on impact, leaving him unconscious.

The third stepped back. He looked back toward the park, then down at his injured comrades.

"What about you, huh?" I screamed at him. "You want some too?"

His unexpected reply: a handgun.

I dropped my short-lived-tough guy act and began to plead. "Woah woah! Come on, man, you don't wanna do this. Take the cash-I don't need it."

His hand and trigger finger shook uncontrollably.

"I'm just gonna walk away, okay?" I said. "I don't want anymore trouble, alright? I won't walk through here again. You got my word." I wouldn't walk any-where in this town again, I promised myself – driving hammered was far less risky.

For a second I thought I had him – his hand began

to shake even harder and his face was ripe with trepidation, his eyes were beginning to water – he hadn't chosen this lifestyle willingly. He'd cave to reason and lower the gun any second.

Only he didn't.

My night concluded with two slugs to the chest. It didn't hurt – it was too fast for pain to even register. I heard the shots and then I was on the ground, looking up at the dark, featureless sky, exhaling four times a second. I sounded like a panting dog.

I tilted my head up and looked around. This was the last thing I was ever going to see: Westlake. I caught a glimpse of the gas station, then a dollar store, an adult video store advertising four VHS for $2, a decrepit three-story apartment building surrounded by an eight-foot-tall barbwire fence, a liquor mart and a cold concrete parking garage. It would likely take a week before anyone who cared discovered my body, before that, I'd just be written off by passerby's as a passed out crackhead.

One of the tabloids would snap a postmortem portrait, would that make their front-page?

And then Westlake skewed into a blur, from which I could vaguely watch the punk who shot me drop the piece at my feet and run.

Darkness. A loud humming pitch emitting from the middle of a small white light in the center of a black canvas. The white light flickered, and then it began to expand outwards, quickly overriding the hollow black slate. This was it. This was death.

To my discontent, I didn't see my life flash before me romantically. I didn't see the dramatic, glistening gates of heaven or the intoxicating, furious fires of hell. I didn't see my grandparents, the ones who had stayed and died over in the old country, or my eldest brother, Matt, whose body they found in the Don Valley Ravine, the back of his head blown off. I'd didn't see anything I wanted to see.

I just saw a noose, crudely tied together from a computer's patch cord, hanging from a cold steel pipe, swinging rhythmically from side to side.

And then, there was nothing.

CHAPTER SIX

THE "EXPERTS" WOULD later tell me that I was clinically dead for two and a half minutes.

When I came to, she was over top of me. Stephanie, sublime as ever, draped in white silk, an angel. But she was always beautiful – five foot eleven, body perfectly toned from the marathons she ran each summer, long dark brown hair and emerald green eyes, topped off by a tendency to lick her lips every time she was excited.

"Sean? Sean?"

"Hey, babe."

"It's okay. You're in a hospital, but I'm here, okay? You were shot, but they operated and you're going to be okay." She was clenching my hand, tears ripe in her eyes.

"How did I get here?"

"Baby. Don't talk. Just rest, okay? Everything is going to be fine. I'm going to take care of you, okay?"

We'd been together for a year, and things had been great, on paper. She was a doctor, a cardiologist (I think) and as such had always been the voice of reason and logic in our relationship. She was good for me.

Aside from my recent binging streak, she had managed to keep me grounded. But despite our theoretical compatibility, there remained the fact that she was almost too composed, too sensible for someone as emotional and stubborn as myself. She would make a great wife one day, no doubt, a great mother too, but she was never the actress stealing scenes in my dreams.

And as always, she kept her promise, patiently nursing me back to health over the next several months, selflessly, with every free instant she had. Yet as my physical wounds healed, my emotional recovery seemed far more skewed; I couldn't sleep, I couldn't relax, my defenses were constantly on code red, and so, the thirst began to grow exponentially.

But beyond this new anxiety, the ordeal served as a harsh wake-up call. I needed to get my act together and for now that meant my deadline. I needed to quit burning time and get back into the game. This was L.A., the most ruthless city on the planet and in its relentless, ever more competitive world of creative writing, even an attempt on your life couldn't buy you an extended timeline.

"This is all good, Sean, real good-trust me. You'll have plenty of time now to brainstorm that final fifteen thousand without distraction. Hell, I figure with so much focus, you should be able to deliver a few weeks early!" Mark had proclaimed, not even bothering to ask how I was feeling.

Come to think of it, this is one business where you really can be worth more to your stakeholders dead than alive.

A relationship? Not so much.

"I love you, Sean" she said softly as we lay in bed one night. The dropping of her trademark professional tone could only mean one thing.

"You too, Steph."

She rested her head on her elbow and looked me over hypnotically, studying me, smiling the whole time. "So, babe. Have you given any thought to what we talked about?" Bingo.

"You're really asking me this now?"

"Well, you've had nothing but time to think."

"Steph, it's like I said, I'm just not ready. Okay? I'm sorry."

She dropped the pleasant gaze and started to grit her teeth. She grabbed my pillow out from under my head and threw it to the floor. "Fine! You can sleep on the couch until you think you are!"

"What?" It was my condo, it was my bedroom, it was my king size. Who the hell did she think she was?

"Go on! Get out!" she screamed, pushing me toward the edge of the bed. She wanted me to stay and fight so that she could try and finally win, but I was way too tired. I just grabbed the pillow off the floor and made my way out into the living room. She locked the door right behind me.

I had a Tiffany's engagement ring, purchased from their store on New York's Fifth Avenue, secure inside a safety deposit box at a bank in Beverly Hills. But the thought of exchanging it for what she could give me in turn just didn't sit. I'd told her many times that I wasn't ready for marriage, yet even though she claimed I was the love of her life, she just couldn't seem to accept this. Like a lot of women nearing thirty, she was in a furious rush, she had told me she only had a year left until she would have to get her eggs frozen as a precaution.

But her parents had been happy – they'd celebrated their fortieth anniversary the year before. I, on the other hand, knew what it meant to land the wrong person. Before I committed, I was going to be 100 percent sure.

Each morning she asked me if I had thought things over and come to my senses, and each morning I told her I hadn't, so I spent the nights of the next two weeks lying awake on the Italian sofa unable to get comfortable enough to actually doze off. Steph had had the thing shipped from Milan for a cool ten grand, but it was like sleeping on a jagged rock. So I spent the nights of the two weeks after that cruising in our six-figure car. The sex appeal of the brand had worn off: now the only thing about it that got me excited was the heated seats. I cruised down the frantic freeways and empty side streets, through the handful of hoods I was still comfortable enough to venture into after dark: the dull, homogenous ones, the emotionally and physically gated ones, the ones defined by selfish excess, disinterested greed and flashy overabundance.

Cruising had once been a great way to escape, to think, to create, back when I had taken friends' cars out on the York-Durham line back in Ontario. That was a country road with an 80 kilometer-per-hour base speed and almost no traffic lights. You could hit 140 and sustain it for a good twenty minutes no problem. It was a great go to when I had a creative block. But out here, driving in a car with way more horsepower on bigger roads with higher speed limits, I felt nothing but emptiness. There was nothing in my head but a constant static. I was a millionaire and it didn't matter. In a capitalist society where wealth is seen as the only true indicator of happiness, that's a pretty scary realization.

"You know? I'm glad this happened to me," I said to Stephanie a few weeks later as we ate lobster at a beach-side restaurant in Malibu. I had told her I wanted to talk; her elegant cocktail dress hinted that she had gotten the wrong impression about what exactly.

She put her hand on my arm and started to blink faster than usual. "What, baby?"

"I'm glad those punks shot me."

She let go of me. "What!"

"I mean, obviously knocking on death's door was a little extreme, but you know, it really cleared some things up for me." And it had. It had brought on an epiphany-a delayed one but profound none-the-less. I wanted to share it with her. I needed to. Whether she ever got a ring from me or not was going to weigh heavily on her reaction.

She crossed her arms. What are you talking about Sean? How many painkillers did you take today?"

Five, but that was beside the point. "I finally understand-why I've had writer's block, why I haven't been able to finish anything."

"Why?" She didn't get it. She never got it-it had been stupid of me to assume this time would be any different. She was wired so differently from me. She didn't live her life through passionate extremism. "Balance" was not a word in my vocabulary. If you wanted something, you went all in. Safe bets were great for pensioners who ate dinner at 3:30 PM. But I still had my real teeth.

I should have quit there, but I carried on. I didn't want to regret losing this one, the way I had so many others before her. If this was going to end, I was going to know I gave it a fair shot. Regrets are the most destructive debt a person can carry. "It's so fitting." I said. "This kind of stuff never used to happen to me. And I never used to have any kind of creative block. I only got mugged because of the suit, the phone, the expensive crap I never had before, back when I first broke out, back when I was actually a great writer."

She shrugged her shoulders and gave me a cold stare. "I don't get it." Nothing had resonated.

"Look at the way we live, Steph." I pointed around the room. At the ocean view, the crystal chandeliers, the $10,000 dollar bottles of wine, the waiters in full suits tending to the needs of pathetic saps who couldn't manage to pull out their own chairs or unfold their own napkins.

She looked around as well, but was entirely content in her surroundings. "What about it?"

"We've got a three-million-dollar condo with a freaking doorman, as if I can't open a damn door for myself, two luxury cars we can't even drive past 50 on these parking lots we have for freeways, a sail-boat down at the marina that we've only used like twice-- I mean we both get seasick, for Christ's sake. All this stuff. All this unnecessary materiality."

"You love all that stuff! It was you that bought it, Sean, remember?"

And yes, I did remember, buying the things my father could never have provided us. The things I wanted to flaunt in his face, even if he was already dead. And I'd had my fun, stroked my ego. But consumerism is a lot like drinking. The more you have, the more you need in order to feel gratification. Now the toys were nothing more than drab expenses. I either needed to buy a jet, or renounce the game altogether.

I took a break, poured myself a new glass of wine and took a large gulp. "Yeah I did buy it. It's been hampering me. Distracting me! See? I've been too spoiled, too pampered. Writing is a starving man's game. When I sold my books I was down to my last dollar. It was succeed or die. But now I haven't had any real motivation because I haven't had any real pressure to deliver."

She gave me this crude glance, as if I'd just stepped on her foot. "That's ridiculous, Sean. You live in a healthy, stable environment. It's your drinking that's been holding you back! If you could just let me help you sober up, then you could start writing again, the way you used to. Alcohol hinders so many things!"

"Steph, trust me. It's not that, okay? Most writers drink-most do far worse than that, actually." Cocaine and acid had long since been staples of the creative writing diet. I didn't like either. Coke made me too frantic to sit still and acid forced me to confront memories I had done everything in my power to repress. I'd heard that meth was the new rage for young authors. I'd even heard of some drinking antifreeze. Whatever works.

"So what are you getting at?" She demanded.

"I need to get back to basics! I need to get out of this town! I haven't written anything decent since I got here!"

"So where do you wanna go?" She wanted me to say something sexy like Paris or Palm Springs. But there was only one city that could save me at this point.

"Back home." I said.

She grabbed her wine glass and took an uncharacteristically large gulp. "For how long?"

"I dunno. I just know I always wrote so well there. Maybe until I finish this one? And it might just be good for me, to get out of L.A. Especially with everything that's happened."

She smiled and clasped my hand firmly in hers. "Baby, you can write well anywhere. What city you're in makes no difference."

She didn't get it. I knew it wasn't her fault, and yet it disgusted me.

"Yes, actually, it does." I said, aggressively. "It's not a science, Steph. It's not like medicine. It's all about mood, about atmosphere. I can't really even explain it. I'm sorry."

She tossed my hands away and went back to crossing her arms "Well, what about us? I mean, I can't go with you. My work's here, Sean!" If it was Paris, she would have quit in a second.

"Maybe you could find new work in Toronto, or just hang out with me there. I've still got plenty to take care of us, and seriously, I think you would love it there! If you would just give it a chance."

She hissed. "In Canada? No thanks." She had once said that it was just too small and backwards a place for her, she who hailed from a town of 2500 in Montana.

So then arose the ever dreaded question: the writing or the woman? For nearly every writer, the answer was crystal clear.

"Okay, well. How 'bout this? I'll just go for a few months or something, I'll get everything just right, focus, hammer out what's left, then I can come back, sell it, everything will be golden, just like it used to be!"

She rolled her eyes and didn't give herself but a second to think things over.

"Sean, if you go to Toronto. I won't be waiting for you when you come back." She kept talking, passionately ranting, but I shut her out. That sentence was all I needed to hear. This was over. I felt strangely relieved.

On the drive home, she screamed and she cried. I didn't listen. I took her back to the condo and told her to have all her stuff out in a week. I packed a light bag and I went straight to LAX.

By the time I reached the gate, I had five missed calls and ten texts from her. I promised myself then and there that I wouldn't look at any of them.

Since making the money, the women had come and gone. There had been seven serious girlfriends in the last four years: whether they had ever wanted me or just the picture on the book jacket remained open to debate.

PART II

September 2011

Toronto, Ontario

CHAPTER SEVEN

Toronto.
Home.

WHENEVER THE MEDIA asked me why I'd left, I told them it had been to further my career. The opportunities for us in the big time were concentrated in the United States-New York or Los Angeles. The latter, the bipolar jungle where I'd turned the three striving manuscripts I'd written while broke and hungry as an undergrad at the University of Toronto into bestselling novels. All the most successful entertainers had left Canada. It was the popular answer to give.

But it was only partially true.

I hadn't been back in five years and that had been deliberate.

As I walked off the plane and made my way towards customs, I remembered the last time I had been in this airport and the promise I had made to myself – the promise to never return.

Of course, there had been my father, memories of him still radiated out from his plot in Mount Pleasant cemetery and the closer I was to it, the more potent the recollections became. The Los Angeles smog blocked the stars, but it had also blocked out most of his lingering presence. There had been entire months in The Southland where he hadn't even come to mind.

And then of course there was? There was what?

Don't you remember? Whispered a stranger residing within a suburb of my subconscious.

No.

My mind showed me nothing more than static, a burning film reel. My father hadn't been enough to drive me from this city, but I couldn't remember much else negative about this place other than him.

And yet, I felt this incredible burning in the pit of my stomach, it wasn't indigestion from the five scotch miniatures I'd kicked back on the plane, it was genuine dread.

You should be fucking terrified.

Of what?

* * *

I hadn't expected him of all people to show up at the terminal, though I was in no position to complain. It felt great to see a familiar face, even if it was his. We'd had had bad blood, my brother Nick and I, since well before my departure-ever since our common enemy had died, really.

We were just too different.

While I had done everything in my power to abandon my roots, he had sought to further embrace them. I wanted to be nothing like my father, he had once said the same. Now he was his spitting image.

He was much shorter than me, only about five-foot-nine and he was in incredible shape. He hit the gym daily and every muscle was well defined. While I wore a suit, he wore baggy low-rise jeans and a track jacket. His head was shaved and his face was covered in rough stubble. On his neck he had the tattoo of the Irish flag and he did his best to imitate an Irish accent.

While I had wanted to be successful, he had wanted the path of least resistance. He lived off me, sucking away at my generosity like a pubic tick. And while I was often tempted to squash him, I always came to my senses. He was family.

"Well well, look who it is. Captain Hollywood! " He said.

"How's it going, Nick?" I moved in to hug him only to have him roughly push me away.

"Was just fucking peachy till I heard you were coming back."

"Always did enjoy your warm receptions, Nick."

"Get your ass in the car. I don't got all day." Not even a handshake. Even still, by our standards, this interaction was going fairly well.

I hustled into the passenger side of his beat up hatchback ripe with 200 000 km, pushing aside an old sandwich, an empty beer bottle and a "used" porn mag to make seating room. I got a closer look at him: his skin was paler, his scars more numerous and his arms were ripe with small needle marks. He wasn't a diabetic.

"So what's new Nick." I asked. "How's everything been?" I didn't really need to ask, I knew he was terrible. He was always in a rut. What I could never figure out was why?

He didn't bother to respond to the question. I doubt he even listened. He never seemed to listen. "So look." He said. "Here's the deal. I'll get ya down to Yorkville, rich bastard like you can find something to his liking there. Won't be like Hollywood, but it's the best us simple Canadian's can do." L.A. celebrities never stray from Yorkville when they're in town. It has everything they need: upscale shopping, five-star restaurants and hotels, and swanky bars. All spread out over a couple of main avenues gridlocked with luxury cars and narrow "aspiring-cobblestone" alley-ways reminiscent of Western Europe. That said it's also filled with balding banking executives fighting through their midlife crises and the shallow skanks who live to bleed them dry. It was Beverly Hills with half the class and twice the pretention. Anyone who actually knew Toronto knew better.

I shook my head and exhaled. "God, Nick. If you were gonna just be a prick, why bother to even pick me up, huh?"

"Mom asked me to. Unlike some of us, I still do what I can to make her happy." We took the ramp onto the 407 expressway. He lifted his transponder from the dash to the windshield for it to register, seemingly unaware that it was broken in half, it didn't beep, and he began to relentlessly curse it.

"You feeling okay, Nick?" I asked. I knew he wasn't, what I didn't know was at this moment, whether he was on cocaine, meth or heroin. I crossed my fingers for cocaine.

He rolled down the window and tossed the transponder out onto the highway. "Fucking piece of shit!" He screamed out after it.

He turned his attention back to me. "I'm nice and dandy, Sean! Not all of us need some high priced shrink to cry to." He looked at me, his eyes wide, his teeth grinding, it was the same stare I used to give to my father behind his back. It was a look of total revulsion.

"Alright, Nick. What's your problem? Huh? You don't answer my calls. You don't come out to visit. And now, you're throwing a tantrum like a five year old. What's going on?"

He reached under the seat and retrieved a flask. "Like you don't know?" He took back a large gulp. "You greedy prick."

"Greedy? Last time I checked I was paying your way."

I sent a care package back to him and mum each year. She had an excuse-she was fifty and sick.

He took another swig and then, not bothering to check his mirror, steered the car from the center lane over to the shoulder, nearly sideswiping a minivan in the process.

"What the hell!" I reached over to grab the wheel from him. He pushed me back into my seat and then slammed on the non-ABS brakes.

I made out with the dashboard-when it kisses, it bites. I could taste the blood, smell it too. My vision was blurry, but that quickly cleared. As I felt for cuts on my forehead, he took another gulp from the flask.

"Paying my way? With that? Those scraps you toss to us?" Two hundred grand a year is scraps?

"Scraps?"

"Yeah, fucking scraps! Compared to what you got! Nice to know you don't think shit about your family! Guess it's hard to remember us now that you live like a king in Hollywood!"

And despite my desire to mend things with him- my previous New Year's resolution, I lost it on him.

Looking back now, I realize just how much I enjoyed our fights, just as I enjoyed bearing witness to his self-destruction. I know he felt the same way about me. In hating each other, we somehow came to love ourselves.

"Okay, first, Hollywood isn't a nice neighborhood anymore, so stop talking about it like its Monaco and I don't live there! I live Downtown, read my emails for once! Second, I'm the one carrying this family, got it? Me. And it's always been me. I was the one busting my ass growing up, while you just burned your life away. I was the one who got a scholarship, while you dropped out at sixteen to collect a welfare check! You know what you're problem is, Nick? You think the world owes you something. You just expect things to fall into your lap. But you know what? Doesn't work that way. I did well, I'll even go so far as to say I got lucky along the way. But don't you ever tell me that you deserve anything from me. If it weren't for mum I wouldn't send you anything. Maybe then for once in your life you'd learn what it's like to actually take responsibility for yourself." The rant left me out of breath, but I could feel the endorphins roaring through my body. I wanted him to counter me. I wanted to bring down another foundation beam in this dwindled relationship.

But he didn't argue, he shut up, finishing what was left of the flask as he silently sulked.

"Get the fuck out. You can walk for all I care." He finally said.

"Fine" I replied, hopping out onto the side of the furious expressway. "Thanks for the ride."

He merged back onto the highway without bothering to close the passenger door. As he gained speed, it became fully ajar, flinging itself into the parallel lane. He didn't seem to notice.

He was the reason I had stashed my mother in a condo in Montreal, knowing damn well he'd never work up the initiative to go out of province to visit her. The thought of him even in the same city as her made me sick to my stomach.

Chapter Eight

I HATE CABS – haven't taken one in years.

So after walking back to the airport, I grabbed a shuttle bus. It dropped me off in front of a ritzy hotel on Front Street, right in the heart of Downtown.

The city was electric. The sidewalks were packed: with tourists looking for a good shot of the CN tower, suits hustling to their next meeting and panhandlers trying to sell TTC transit tokens. They were here now and they'd be here after dark, when they would be joined by the suburban bar crowd heading to The Esplanade and its patios. They say you can gauge a city by the health of its downtown. Toronto was in great shape.

I found a payphone in Union Station and called Adam Li, a childhood friend and former literary collaborator to let him know I was back in town. He told me to swing by for drinks.

He lived in a two-bedroom top floor apartment (he called it a penthouse, it most certainly was not) on Davisville in Midtown. He'd been there, locked in since graduation with his wife: the only woman he'd ever seen naked. The apartment was unspectacular, save for a huge 3D TV. Married people don't have sex, they watch reality TV.

"I love the view from up here man." I commented as we sat on his balcony facing south and the vast, multilayered Downtown skyline, sipping on hoppy pints of ice cold Steamwhistle, my favorite Toronto beer. "And it's so nice to actually taste a real brew again, my God, after the watered down junk they sell down south." American beer was to be consumed in shameless excess or not at all.

"Haha, I bet. It's great to see you man! It's been too long!" He was an energetic man, still positive and idealistic, always wearing a smile. It was the byproduct of never having lost his "first love". We got along well. But there were occasions where his straight laced persona agitated me. He wore sweater vests daily, daily! He would have made a great Jehovah's Witness.

"Yeah! What happened to that visit you were gonna make last winter? As I recall I still owe you a Tijuana lap dance? Will blow your mind man, those Mexican girls have the best asses you'll ever see. It's like a lava lamp. I could watch them jiggle all day."

He flicked up his hand and the wedding band. "Ah, Sean. You know how it is. I'm married now. Things aren't always just my decision."

"Or yours at all."

He hesitated in contemplation for a second. "Yeah. Exactly." The final stage of grief is acceptance.

"Nice. So how is wifey anyhow?" I said.

"She's good man! At a teacher's conference in Halifax for the weekend."

"Ah! So that's why you're allowed out!"

He didn't have to think this time. "Yeah. Exactly."

He pulled out his phone and showed me a photo of the two of them standing in front of Niagara Falls. The same uninspired photo every couple has on their Facebook. He wanted me to ask him how he had enjoyed the romantic weekend there, but I wasn't in the mood, so I changed the subject. "How's the book coming?"

He gave me a perplexed expression. "What book?"

I laughed. "You know? The one you told me about last year, the Napoleon time piece? The one you said was gonna be your big break."

"Half-way through."

"Oh, I've heard that one from you before." Five times in fact. Every failed writer is always "half way through". Not a quarter or two thirds, a half, every single time.

"Look. I dunno how you do it man! I can't stay focused. I have this burst of inspiration and I pump out a hundred pages like that! And then another idea comes along and I gotta go and pursue that instead! I got like thirty books half-way finished, just can't seem to close any of them."

I put my hand on his shoulder, the Steamwhistles were stacking up into a skyline at my feet so I was start-ing to get sentimental. "Brother, listen. I can get you published, I really can. I just need a finished product to work with! Come on bud, you're a great writer, help me, help you." I had the contacts, he had the talent. I desperately wanted to put the two pieces together. He was a spayed dog, I held the keys to his cage, but he refused to let me open it.

"I know man and I appreciate it. I really do. I just need some more time. Things have been busy lately, real crazy, you know how it is. Family, work, there just aren't enough hours in the day to write anymore. And me and Janet are thinking about having a baby." What? He was only twenty-seven.

"A baby? Wow. That's a big step." The final nail in the coffin.

"Sure is. But, I think we're both ready to take it. So what about you man? How have you been doing? I can't even imagine what you just went through. Are you okay?"

"Yeah! I'm fine. What doesn't kill you, right?" My body was back to normal, my mind was still a bit screwed up, but whatever, when wasn't it?

"You're tough Sean."

Not tough enough.

"I mean it wasn't on my bucket list, but whatever, good material for a book, right?" I said.

"That's a great way to look at it!"

The conversation lulled. I kept drinking. Adam hit his "three beer limit" and switched over to ginger ale.

"How's the newest book coming, Sean?" He asked to break the short-lived silence.

"Not well man" I replied. "But." I looked out at the skyline and felt a sense of warmth resonate. "I think things are gonna pick up here. L.A. is a great city, but I couldn't even write a decent Haiku out there."

"So you've come back home to rediscover your muse?"

I smiled at the romanticism of it. "Bingo."

"I like that. So what's your plan? Where are you gonna stay? Yorkville? I hear there are some terrific new hotels there."

I slapped him playfully on the back. "Come on! You know me better than that! I just came from L.A., the last thing I need are wannabe snobs. Nah! I was actually thinking of maybe moving back to The Annex. I wanna see if I can find something like our old one bedroom!"

"Really? Do you remember what that place was like?"

Did I remember? I remembered keggers, jello shots and pantless parties. I remembered an era where the only thing that mattered was having enough change left over after buying booze to pull off a condom run. I remembered putting on my headphones and writing effortlessly from dusk to dawn. "Yeah! It was great!" I said. "I need to get back to basics. I've been spoiled way too long."

He nodded awkwardly, not really knowing how to react. "Well. That sounds like an interesting plan. You need anything, just you let me know. Janet and I are here for ya."

"Thanks man. I appreciate it."

"No worries man, it's great to have you back."

And as we sat there, on the rust plagued, disintegrating balcony covered in empty beer bottles and shattered dreams, twenty stories north of Yonge Street- the city's largest artery, I had the most pleasant surge of déjà vu. It was an invigorating sensation I so dearly wanted to grasp onto and never let go of.

CHAPTER NINE

I COULDN'T BELIEVE MY luck when I found it available, the old creative sweatshop. Our one bedroom on Madison Avenue, pumped into the heart of The Annex, one of the city's youngest, most popular neighborhoods. It was fully furnished with ninth hand junk the previous occupants had likely found on the side of the road and ready to go for $1200 a month, less than my condo's monthly maintenance fee.

All I'd brought back was a small suitcase with a week's worth of clothes and my laptop so unpacking was a non-issue. Looking around the apartment I loved the lack of clutter, it was hard to have a messy home when all you had was a bed, a couch, a desk, and a quarter a closet worth of clothes. The kitchen was stripped bare, even the oven was missing, but it didn't matter, there were so many good take out places in The Annex, I'd never get bored.

And inevitably, for the first time in ages, I truly reminisced about my student years, as I walked the crowded Bloor Street stretch between St George and Bathurst. The strip was riddled with a subtle but soothing cue of artistic pretentiousness, buried miles deep, under its diverse, vibrant mosaic: crackheads, students and yuppies were each given an equal slate.

Reminiscing, of simpler times, better times, when The Dream was enough to subside all the pain in the world, without having to resort to a single drop. I'd spent four fantastic years in this neighborhood: smoking grass with strangers on the rooftop patio of The Maddy – the area's student dominated pub, hitting on busty sorority girls at the frat house keggers I frequently crashed, shopping for bargains on my favorites authors at the three floored BMV bookstore and receiving sloppy blow jobs from dates over in Queens Park – the home of the provincial government, always conveniently abandoned after dark. It was a great neighborhood, a wonderful place to be young and ambitious. Though, I was no longer either of those things.

So thirsty…

So I stopped into Restless, a low key lounge on the southeast corner of Bloor and Bathurst over by Honest Ed's-the thrift superstore and premiere Toronto landmark where I had bought all my clothes prior to selling my first book.

The bar was packed: a lot of good looking grad students were there on awkward first dates, sitting across from one another at two person tables drinking red wine over candlelight. At the bar itself, a bunch of pathetic lonely old men were getting their jollies chatting with a young bleach blonde bartender with huge fake tits. She threw out a smile to them every time she received an order.

I walked quickly past both groups of people and took a seat at the very back of the bar, in a dark lonely corner right next to the DJ booth which was blaring mellow jazz.

I got comfortable on one of the joint's velvet couches and began admiring the abstract artwork hanging on the walls. One painting in particular caught my attention: it had a bright red humanoid figure overtop a black background. He was a holding a bottle, his mouth wide open as if he was belching. His eyes were hollow and they followed you, maintaining eye contact no matter what angle you approached it from. When I turned away from it, I could feel it watching me and when I looked at it again I could swear I saw it wink.

"Hey Sweetie, you having a good night?" A waitress asked me. A young brunette with perky tits and layers of makeup. She was desperately artificial and yet I couldn't help but find her sexy. She knew it too. She carried an aura of superiority, the kind a woman would assemble after being hit on a few thousand times. Toronto was the pickup capital of the world-she got propositioned fifty times a day.

"Yeah." I instinctively smiled only to pull myself back to a conservative smirk. I'd seen her approach the tables sporting couples with a cold disinterest. I wasn't going to play the game. I see through you waitresses now. I see you for who you really are. Your tip is 15 percent, period. Spare me the stupid recital. Let's just get down to business.

I watched the men at the bar. They were begging the blonde to give them each a hug. She laughed the request off and then gave two of them a demeaning pat on the head. Both of the guys blushed from the contact. She asked them to order something top shelf and they eagerly requested the most expensive scotch in the house, it was about $40 a shot. It earned them each a pinched cheek. I didn't know whether to laugh or pity them.

Maybe this was the way all women saw men: wallets and tips. It had been a long time since I'd dated a girl who didn't know my net worth to the very figure.

The waitress told me her name but I didn't bother to pay attention.

"What can I get for you, hun?"

"A pitcher of Mill Street." A solid Toronto beer.

"Two glasses?" She asked.

"One."

She hesitated for a second.

"What? Don't tell me it's a two person minimum on the pitcher. I can drink it out of two glasses if that makes any difference." Some of the prissier bars insisted as such.

"No! That's fine." She said. "Sorry, it's just. You look really familiar. Where have I seen you?"

Chance of bedding her, 90 percent. It had been a while for me. I couldn't wait to tear off her panties with my teeth. If she was wearing panties at all.

"Well, tell me, are you a big reader?" I said, playfully.

She laughed, letting out a repulsive snort. "Um no! Haven't touched a book since high school! God all that crap was so boring! Right?"

Interest in bedding her, 0 percent.

She smiled and snapped her fingers. "Wait. I got it! You play for the Canucks, don't you?! Defenseman? Second line?"

"Sure" I had no idea what she meant at first, and then I remembered: Vancouver Canucks-NHL-hockey-Canada's game-gotcha. Back in Los Angeles, hockey found itself relegated to a small blurb on page ten of the sports section, next to cricket or lawn bowling. I wasn't even sure where the Kings played, was anyone in L.A. sure? The Staples Center? I'd lived a three minute walk from it for over two years and had never noticed anything but Laker jerseys.

"Oh my God! Can I have your autograph?" She stopped looking directly at me, her cheeks turned rosy red.

"Sure."

She reached through her pockets for a piece of paper but came up short.

"No! As if! I never have any luck!" She pouted.

I reached into my wallet and pulled out an American fifty, which I quickly scribbled a signature on, in the hopes that it would make her go away.

"Here." I handed it towards her.

"No! I couldn't take that!"

"Go for it." Hurry up with the drinks already!

She walked over to the bar and to my frustration, grabbed a black marker instead of the pitcher.

"I'll probably get in shit for this, but what the hell?" She said. "How often do I get to see one of you guys in the flesh!" She pulled her tank top down a few inches and pressed her impressive bust together for me to John Hancock.

"You can grab a feel too, if you want." She added.

* * *

I drank three pitchers and began to feel a wave of nausea crash over me. The music slowed, the room darkened. Patrons became flashes of light. On the couch next to me a group of yuppies were lighting fire to some Sambuca. I began to sweat.

I asked for some water. They say if you consume a glass per drink you'll never go wrong.

I drank three glasses. Things calmed down.

I grabbed two more pitchers and kept pounding back pints until I was past all of my fears, my insecurities, my inhibitions. And then I got the intense craving, even stronger than that for sex – to jot down another chapter in my long awaited "masterpiece." It was the most gratifying feeling imaginable.

Hell yes! It's on!

I had to hurry, like an erection in a senior citizen, this kind of focus was both rare and short lived.

I paid the bill in cash and hustled out into the cool September night, completely ignoring the waitress's desperate request that I call her-via the digits she had left on the bill. I knew so little about hockey, she would have seen through me before I even managed to get her bra off.

And then, time stopped.

The furious street went silent.

The guitars held by the buskers no longer echoed chords, the desperate pleas from the homeless no longer irritated, the gridlock on the road cleared. I could no longer feel the cold. When I rubbed my head I couldn't feel that either. My body had gone completely numb. The confusion, the fear, the inner turmoil all vanquished, overwritten by a soothing ember which began in my stomach but rapidly spread the expanse of my body.

The pause button had been pressed. The city was a painting, a private viewing for me alone.

Steps away from the historic Bloor Cinema I caught a glimpse of HER. SHE was the only thing moving against the static backdrop.

SHE was dressed in a grey Ryerson Hoodie and faded blue jeans.

HER long black hair flew harmonically with the nonexistent wind.

HER majestic green eyes emitted a soothing ultra-violent beam directly into my fragmented soul.

HER skin was pale white and luminous.

HER open mouth revealed HER perfectly straight shiny white teeth.

SHE hadn't aged a day.

SHE smiled at me and I was too nervous to do anything in response.

SHE blew me a kiss.

It was then I realized, I didn't remember HER name.

SHE walked into the cinema. There was some sort of TIFF event being held and I could see SHE was holding a ticket.

A CAR HORN. It made me jump.

Bloor was full of cars, cabs and bikes once more. I felt myself shiver from the brisk evening air and a bunch of drunken frat boys had begun brawling outside the dive bar next to Restless.

I jaywalked across the street and made my way towards the cinema. I wanted to catch HER before SHE got to HER seat.

When I got to the entrance, an usher closed the door and put himself in front of it.

"Ticket, sir?" He asked.

"No. Could I buy one now?" I replied

"Sorry sir, we're full up."

"Could I just run in real quick? I need to say hi to a friend."

"Sorry sir, no ticket, no entry."

"Do you have any idea who I am? Go tell your manager Sean O'Connor wants a ticket." I barked aggressively.

"Sir, I have no idea who you are. And this is a closed event, I'm sorry."

I pulled out my wallet. "Okay, how much do you want? I have $200 in cash. But I can make a bank run if need be." I truly didn't care how many pieces of wrinkled paper I had to do away with.

"Sir, this is a closed event, there are no more tickets for sale, at any cost." At any cost? I'd never heard something so obscene.

I thought about waiting around for the movie to end, but that prospect, even in my own head, sounded far too creepy to execute.

By the time I got home the inspirational fire had died out, replaced only with ashes of disorientation.

Chapter Ten

I'VE NEVER BEEN to Ireland.

It's on my bucket list, right up there with have a threesome and drink a fifty year old bottle of wine.

They say Galway is the best city, the people are supposed to be lovely.

It was where my mother had been born and she was an angel, a proper catholic gal without a selfish bone in her body. It was never about her. It was always about the family. It was a virtue she had always tried to instill in me.

"Dad's going out to the hardware store. You should go with him, Sean. Spend a little time with him." She had said one Saturday morning in the fall of 1995. I was eleven: sitting at the kitchen table getting my fix of sugary cereal, eager to get outside and play basketball with some friends.

"Why?" I replied. Friday nights were always his hardest, most Saturdays he was an emotionless zombie, barely capable of carrying on even the most basic of conversations as he stumbled from his bedroom to the bathroom, one turbulent round-trip after another.

"Because I'm telling you too! Because it would be good for you two to have some one-on-one time, get to know each other better." She insisted.

"I have to?"

"You have to. Do it for me, please? You love your mum, don't ya?" Her accent was so musical – it could make even the most repulsive premise sound absolutely charming.

"Fine."

She gave me a firm hug and a kiss on the forehead. "Good boy. Have fun!"

It was 10 am, so I was shocked when the stench struck me the second I opened the passenger door. It was bourbon alright. He very rarely drank in the mornings, but there were always exceptions.

"You ready to roll, tough guy?" He said through slurred speech. His eyes were blood red, his entire body jittery – he was still on the peak of his own personal Everest, yet to make the rough descent with no remaining canisters of oxygen. He must have started at the break of dawn, or maybe he was running a marathon, still going strong from the night before.

I thought about turning and walking away, but I wanted to see my mother smile, at any cost, she never did anymore. I could see her, watching through the front window on the verge of a grin. "Yeah, let's do it." I said to him, getting in and immediately buckling up.

I minded my business as he ran stop signs, changed multiple lanes without signaling and accelerated to nearly triple the speed limit. There were constant horns and middle fingers but no sirens, he was always extremely lucky when it came to the police.

"You see that new Rebecca girl, just moved in down the street?" He asked me. I had, she was a few years older than me and very cute. But I was way too young to care.

"No sir."

"She's this cute little blond. What a sweet ass, my God. Mother of Mary! Get on that before Nick does, Sean. It's your turn, so take it, don't want you to end up a faggot." His accent wasn't musical like my mother's – it was vile and cruel, just like him. The strength of it positively correlated to how much he had drank. There were times where I couldn't understand a single word he said, those were the scariest of all. You'd just have to guess: say yes or no at random and then silently pray.

"Yeah. I will. I'll tap her real good." I replied.

Golden rule: when they're drunk, agree with everything they say, it's the best way to avoid an outburst.

He ran his hand through my hair playfully. "That's my boy. Well, my man.

You're growing up fast."

"Yeah, sure am."

"Fuck, enjoy it while you can, Sean. It's all downhill from there. Really is. What I wouldn't give to be young again, young and back in Dublin."

He turned the car unexpectedly.

"Isn't the hardware store down?" I pointed out the obvious, now in the other direction.

He ignored the observation "Yeah, all the women I would fuck, if I was young again, I'd go blind. If I didn't have that bitch of a ball and chain holding me down." He was so lucky to have my mother but he'd never get it. I'd seen photos of her as a teenager back in Galway and she had been stunningly beautiful. Now, she just looked frail, sick, elderly, even if she was only in her mid-thirties. He'd beaten the vitality right out of her, her soul right out of her. She was already a decaying corpse.

"Ball and chains suck." Agree with everything they say.

"But there's no hope of that, it's all over for me now. It's just gonna be further downhill from here," he said.

He drove up onto a rail crossing, known for an abundance of freight trains, slammed on the breaks and put the car into park.

"Dad?"

He looked to the sky and began to rant in a trance like state. "It's just the same bullshit everyday now, there's no reason to get up in the morning anymore. Not even a blowjob on my birthday. I don't give a fuck anymore. I'm sick of it all."

"Dad, move the car please." I begged, as gently as I could.

He looked at me, perplexed. "Huh?"

"The car. Drive off the"

"Shut the fuck up! You wouldn't understand!" He screamed in retort.

"Dad, please." I felt myself starting to shake, I looked to my door, he had already activated the lock, the type you can't handle manually from the inside. Maybe I could smash the window with my elbow?

"Don't be a little bitch, Sean. I raised you to be a

man! Let's have a drink together." He reached into the backseat and pulled out a half empty bottle of

bourbon. He took a giant gulp and then tossed it into my lap. "Go on, have a drink, it'll make it all better, make all the pain just disappear."

The roar, out in the all too near distance.

"Dad."

"Have a fucking drink!" He insisted, clenching his fist.

I could see it now, it was massive, without question it would crush our car like an empty pop can being jumped on by a bodybuilder.

"Dad please!" I could hear the driver sound the horn at us.

My father caught sight of it and laughed. "Come and get me, motherfucker!" He screamed at it. "I'm right here!"

"Dad! Please!" I begged.

He struck me, viciously across the cheek and pushed my head back "God, all you ever do is fucking whine on and on all day like a little bitch, you're worse than your mother!" He screamed, pressing my head back and forcing the neck of the bottle between my teeth, pouring the poison down my unwilling throat. "There you go, Sean, now you're drinking like a real man! Your granddad would be proud."

I choked and frantically panicked as the third ounce made its way into my virgin stomach. The headlights consumed us – you couldn't see anything through the blinding white light.

"Alright, let's roll." He laughed. He let go of me

and shifted the transmission into drive, pounding the pedal.

The train pulled in at full speed and clipped the car's rear bumper as we flew forward. The impact sent us spinning crudely in a complete circle before we came to a harsh stop safely on the other side of the track.

I threw up a little in my hands. I quickly wiped them clean on the inside of my shirt so he wouldn't see.

"Alright, now what did I need from the hardware store? Fuck that, let's go and grab us another beverage instead." He proclaimed, taking another drink from the bottle.

CHAPTER ELEVEN

A DAM AND I sat along the empty second floor bar
of the Wiseman Brewery over by Dundas Square.
It was a beer hall with cheap suds in Bavarian portions.
Guaranteed hangover included at no extra charge.
I was drinking a liter of blonde with a few ounces of
tequila mixed in.

"This area's changed a lot, it's crazy." I said, looking out the window at the massive crowds of tourists and 905'ers (a 905'er=someone from the Toronto
suburbs) down in The Square. They all looked lost as
they walked way too slowly through a shanty town of
overpriced food carts (think giant pretzels and six dollar lemonade) and tacky merchandise stands (selling
I Love Toronto buttons and novelty T-shirts of D-list
celebrities amongst other touristy junk). The ones
who weren't walking were busy taking cheesy photos of themselves in front of the massive advertising
billboards that somehow came to pass as landmarks,
to show their friends back in whatever suburb they
hailed from. All around them, buskers, hustlers and

pick-pockets quested for change while some whackos screamed on and on about the return of Jesus.

There was a time when all that was around the area were strip clubs and porno theaters. Now it was an official stop on the Toronto city bus tour.

"Yeah man, it's Time Square Jr. now. Not bad on the weekends though, always some cool concerts or festival going on." Adam said.

"I remember I came here once with my dad. We went to Massey Hall and saw George Steinman, seventh row." – A popular observational comedian of the nineties.

"Steinman? Wow!"

"Great show, he's one funny son of a bitch. But I remember waiting in line for it on Shutter Street and seeing homeless guys beating each other half to death over a loonie someone had dropped, while a pimp was threating one of his girls with a switchblade. It was nuts." One homeless guy had actually grabbed me, gripped his filthy hands over my throat and told my father he'd break my neck if he wasn't given twenty dollars. My father tossed on his iron knuckles and beat the guy unconscious. The old man had never lost a fight in his life.

"Wow, that must have been scary!"

I shrugged. "Made great writing material."

"But you're right, Toronto's changed. It's really cleaned itself up. There's hardly any bad areas now. Even Scarborough's looking pretty good these days.

"That, I'll have to see to believe." I said skeptically.

"Oh yeah man! Tons of people are moving there from Downtown, it's the only part of the city that's still affordable. Jan and I may even do it down the road." I hated the sound of that: moving back to where you started, it seemed so anticlimactic.

"Anyway, I wanted to ask you. Do you remember a girl who went to Ryerson. Like 5'9? Black hair? Green Eyes? Really cute." I asked him.

"That went to Ryerson? No. I didn't know too many people from there. Who is she?"

"I dunno. I saw HER last night over on Bloor. I know I know HER, I think I've like slept with HER, I saw HER and I just lit up, but I can't even remember HER name. Weird right?"

"Yeah it happens to me too sometimes, I see old friends of friends, people I used to hang out with, years back, but I can't figure out who they are for the life of me. Guess we're starting to get old. Creep Facebook, see if she turns up?"

"Yeah, that's a good idea."

His phone began to vibrate, the whole time he had had it out in front of him, the volume maxed. He was always on call: a "doctor" waiting for an over dramatic emotional "emergency".

"Sean, sorry I gotta take this."

"Go for it, Romeo."

He was terrified the second he put the phone to his ear "Hey Darling! How are you? Baby! I told you, I'm out with Sean, he's back in town, we're just having a drink. Baby! What's wrong? Yes, I told you about it, I even wrote it on the whiteboard. I did! It's right there! Dinner with Sean! Okay, I'm sorry baby. No, I didn't mean to be cheeky! No! I'm sorry okay! I'll be home soon. An hour okay? No? Thirty minutes? No? Okay,

I'll be home in fifteen. Yeah. Yeah I swear. Okay, love you sugarplum, bye bye."

"Did I get you in trouble?" I smirked. My visitation rights were being stripped little by little with each passing year. Once they get married, they fade into the distance, one anniversary at a time. It wasn't just him – all my other guy friends had married off too. The rest lived in the 905 and contact with them was limited to a Facebook message on my birthday. Messages their wives would edit before they were allowed to press send.

"Ah no. It's okay. You know how Jan is. She likes to check in, make sure I'm okay. But I really do need to get home, get the apartment ready for Jan's parents. They're visiting in a few days from Hong Kong."

I checked my phone. "It's only 9:30? That's a pretty tight curfew you've got going on. She's got you on quite the leash."

"Ah you know, it's all good. I'm a very lucky guy, Sean. Luckiest guy alive. I know you may not believe me, but it's all worth it, even if I do have to make some concessions in exchange. You'll understand, once you find the right girl and settle down." And seeing him, a man whipped worse than a racehorse trailing on the last lap, I could see that he was genuinely happy, completely content with his life. He truly was lucky.

"Yeah, we'll see about that." I said, cynically.

"Ah just wait and see. Everyone talks like that when they're single, but then she comes along and everything changes. It'll happen soon, I guarantee it."

The romantic in me wanted so badly to believe in the gospel of his naivety. To trust that there was one person out there who could fix me, complete me. The romantic in me was very vocal and his drawn out dramatic lectures could often drown out the bitter retorts of plentiful experience.

You will find someone, Sean. SHE's still out there. You will find someone and everything will be okay.

I liked the romantic in me. I needed him. He kept me breathing.

Adam cashed out and put his jacket on. "Look, Sean. Before I go. My writers craft class is doing a project on one of your books, *Dead Heart*. I was hoping you could, maybe, if you're not too busy tomorrow?" Ah, *Dead Heart*! It was my first published novel. And while it was the weakest of my three it held a very special place in my heart. You never get over your first.

"Sure man. Would be my pleasure." I said.

"Oh thank you! That would mean so much to me! And to them! To see a real live writer in person and have you talk about the key things we've identified in the book. It would take everything to another level. I can give you a list of the themes we've been discussing if you want? For a little prep?"

"No. It's okay."

"You sure?"

"Adam, I wrote the damn book, remember? I think I'll manage."

I took it upon myself to arrive prepared this time. I picked up a mickey of whiskey and drank it at the back of a TTC bus on the way to Thomas Edison High, a few blocks east of Don Mills. By the time I got there, I was in a great mood. Even the ads on the bus for child suicide were making me laugh.

* * *

The little brats were unanimously disinterested and unimpressed. The girls: ripe with bleach and flavored lip gloss texted their football player boyfriends on their brand new iPhones while the boys tossed paper airplanes and playful jabs back and forth. Adam introduced me to the back wall.

"Guys, we have a very special visitor. A very successful author here all the way from Los Angeles. The writer behind our current novel, a close friend of mine, Sean O'Connor! So let's give him a very warm welcome to Writers 101!"

They clapped, but only because they felt their grade depended on it. It was a bit disheartening. I wasn't used to departed audiences.

"Sean. I'll let you have the floor?" He didn't seem to pick up on the awkwardness of the situation. He always did live life inside his own, picture perfect, warm and fuzzy little world. Sober me would have flipped them off and gone to the bar, but right now I was pumped up, eager to play teacher.

"Let's rock!" I shouted, waking up two in the front row who had already passed out. Unopened energy drinks resting on their desks. When was the last time I had a Jagerbomb?

I dropped the ten minute stock speech. I wasn't under contract.

"Okay. Well. First off. By show of hands. Who here actually gives a fuck about writing?" Adam took a step back and gasped.

The profanity was unexpected and much appreciated as evidenced by a bout of laughter to accompany the single hand lifted. It belonged to a socially awkward outlier in the front row, who didn't seem to be bothered by the onslaught of discerning gazes. He was poorly dressed: in jeans that were too baggy and a shirt with sleeves that were too short. His face was covered in acne and his hair was long and out of control. Of all who made eye contact with me, he was the only one to get uncomfortable. He was the only one to be intimidated. He was the only fan.

"That's what I figured. Who here has actually read my book?" I asked.

Again, only the same single hand.

"Fucking dork." Someone muttered to him, quiet enough to keep it under wraps.

"Sean. This isn't L.A., it's a grade eleven class, keep it together." Adam whispered. As per usual, I didn't bother to listen.

"Now you probably expected me to come in and brag on and on about my book like a jackass. But what's the point? I sold a mill-five copies of it, I know it's good, why bother trying to convince you? I don't need you to buy it or get your little friends to buy it. I'm doing just fine without you. So let's cut the shit and talk about you. I mean, why are you in this class? Wasn't mandatory."

"It's a bird!" A skater shouted out.

"Bird course. Okay. Fair enough. I would 'a taken Psych for that personally. Each their own. Any other reasons?"

Silence.

"No exams!" A fat kid shouted to a few accompanying laughs.

Silence once more.

"Ah. Come on! You're telling me no one here wants to be the next great writer? Make a million over night?" I carried on. Hoping I could find some way to engage them. I don't know why I cared, but I did.

"I know some writers. They live over in Moss Park." A pretty boy retorted to be a wise ass.

"Okay! Sure. There are some losers. But there are plenty of winners too. The richest woman in the U.K is a writer."

"The Queen?" A cheerleader in the back row.

"No! The chick who wrote the *Wizard* books. She's a billionaire. Sells out the ACC just to read a manuscript. That's crazy! The Raptors can't even sell out."

"So you're saying the only reason to be a writer is to get rich?" A nerd in the front.

"No! But it's a perk, no doubt. Among a lot of other things. Critical praise can really get you chubbed."

Some laughter, then silence. Adam looked ready to faint, he was texting furiously, asking wifey for help.

"Okay. Let's try something else. Who here likes Hollywood movies?" I asked.

Every hand, save for the one I expected.

"Okay! Okay! Good! So, who here saw *Heartless* with Courtney Len last year?" Ahh Courtney Len. She had been all the rage. She was a former child star, discovered on a nationwide talent show for her incredible vocal range. But it was the sex tape she had made at eighteen that had truly propelled her to fame, rendering her "worthy" of a leading role in my book's adaptation. She had her throat cut last month, not far from where I was shot actually. Los Angeles-you can't make that shit up.

Every hand, save for one. I was liking that one more by the minute. When I was in high school, I had been that one.

"Sick movie!" Some jock in a football jersey yelled out.

"Really? What did you like about it?" I asked him.

"Len was smoking." He replied.

"Okay. No argument there. Anything else?"

"The ending was badass!" A stoner in the back.

"Well, I guess by Hollywood standards. I liked my ending a lot better." I countered.

"You wrote that movie?" The stoner asked.

"No man, I wrote the book!"

Silence.

"Seriously?" I tapped lightly on *Dead Heart's* front cover: one of the original covers that featured the Toronto skyline. Every version released in the last few years was a movie tie in with Len's tits front and center.

"It was based on that?" A ditsy brunette asked.

How had Adam not told them this already? Then again why did he even need to? It used to be, you read a book then you saw the movie. Then it became you saw a movie then read the book. Now I guess it was you streamed the movie online and the only thing you read were your friend's comments on it via Twitter. How sad a state. A lot of great writers died broke while YouTube videos of babies burping gathered a hundred million views.

"No shit! But the book's way better. Way grittier.

Movie was toned down for that pussy 14A rating. Henry doesn't just get shot, he gets torn in half by a subway on the University Line oh and there's an orgy. Chapter nine, page 83."

The guys in the room perked up and promptly flipped to the page in question.

I hated the orgy scene, it was gratuitous and completely unnecessary to the story, but Hanson had assured me it would get us plenty more attention. The masses didn't care for allegory, but they could always make time for double penetration.

* * *

After the bell rang and the room had emptied, Adam took me aside.

"Sean, what the heck was that? You didn't even talk about the themes of the book! I was trying to show them that even in contemporary fiction there's real depth and meaning! All you did was highlight the snuff!"

"Ah come on. At least they'll read it, well some of them now. When the hell did you become so rigid, I though you always wanted to be the 'cool' English teacher?" I retorted.

"I am a cool English teacher. But I don't have to sink to their level or apparently yours. They were just playing up for you. A lot of them do actually care. We did *The Great Gatsby* last month, they got pretty involved." I remembered my twelfth grade class, I had read *The Great Gatsby* three times in a dedicated effort to derive all possible meaning from that masterpiece, the rest had just skimmed the Sparknotes website and watched the trailer for the 1974 film.

"Adam, get real, they don't care. Nothing you say or do here is gonna change that. You need to get the hell out of this dead-end and do something worthwhile with you time and your talent."

"God, Sean, you started drinking again, didn't you?" He asked me.

"What?"

"All this 'screw it all' nonsense. You're off the wagon again, right? The sober Sean could have gotten through to them without being a prick. The way you always got through to me!" The guy hadn't seen me in almost a year. He had stood me up for visits on two separate occasions under Jan's orders. He didn't have the right to make any accusations.

"Man, it's none of your business and you wouldn't understand. So, just let it go, okay?"

He leaned in to be discrete even though it was an empty room. "Sean. You're one of my best friends. I think of you as a brother, you know that. You can't just expect me to stand by and watch you destroy yourself. If you wanna keep my friendship, get your act together, go get some help. I have a friend in AA, he could sponsor you. Get you back on track man. Let me give you his number."

"Destroying myself? Jesus, don't be so overdramatic! So I like to drink once in a while, who doesn't?"

"It's 2:30 on a Wednesday and you're trashed!"

So? I'm not going to AA! I got better things to do than listen to a bunch of losers bitch on about their problems!"

"They're not losers, Sean. They're people trying to better themselves. A lot of them are just like you."

"Like me? Christ, way to be condescending. I'm not going to AA! I'm fine."

So I was drinking a little more than usual? Big deal. Alcoholism was a North American invention. In Ireland and Scotland they just called it "having a good time." Plus, statistics showed our generation was drinking less than any other in recorded history. What we called binging our ancestors would have thought of as a pre-drink.

"Sean, you're a real asshole sometimes, you know that?" He said and then he stormed off while texting.

"What! Come on! Be a man, don't go running to wifey! Talk to me for Christ sake!" He ignored me all the way to his next class.

* * *

As I waited for a bus back Downtown the outlier approached me. His body language was tense and constricted. He was nervous of me, the way most "normal" Canadian teens are of movie stars or hockey players.

"Mr. O'Connor?"

"Hey! What's going on, man?"

"My names, Nate. Nate Rode. I wanted to let you know, I actually read your book."

"Oh yeah? Right on. And what did you think? Honestly."

"Um, I really liked it. Behind all the violence, I thought it was a really fascinating look at social conflict in conservative Western societies and the erosion of the middle class. I saw the movie too, but it completely missed the mark, because it didn't feature any of that, just the tits and explosions." I liked the way he said it, he spoke really well for a sixteen year old.

"Wow! That's pretty spot on, you read that online?"

"No. I don't plagiarize ideas." He replied assertively.

"Well then I'm impressed, maybe you should be teaching this class."

"Well, I always try and read between the lines. It's good practice. I'm a writer too actually." No way! I thought we were going extinct.

"Rocking. Welcome to the sick and twisted family. You written anything major yet?"

"Um, not a novel yet, no. But I was wondering. If maybe, if you have the time, if you could have a look at a novelette of mine? Just for some feedback? I would really appreciate it."

He reminded me so much of myself at that age. "Yeah. Sure kid. Why not? I can give it a peek. You want my email?"

"I have it on a stick, actually, my email's written on the side." He replied handing me over a USB key.

"You come prepared, I like that. Alright, Nate. Give me a week or so."

"Thanks so much Mr. O'Connor, I really appreciate it! Thanks again!"

I wouldn't admit it, but, the exchange made my day.

CHAPTER TWELVE

AFTER THE SHOOTING, I began making myself a cup of tea every night, partially to wash down the bitter aftertastes and partially in some ill-fated attempt to relax my nerves. I started with a simple herbal lemon, then switched over to chamomile, then some dodgy Chinese blend, then I started spiking it with 151 (75.5 percent white rum in case you didn't know). I just wanted to sleep. I just couldn't "shut off".

I sat in front of my Mac, in that lonely, poorly lit apartment (there was only one light in the main room and it flickered constantly, even after I put a brand new bulb in the socket). The paint on the walls peeled away, as it did, small pieces of dry wall crumbled and fell down to the worn, stained carpet, which hadn't been vacuumed in about five years. The drain pipes gargled, and the ants scurried, while I hit the backspace key with equal frequency to all others combined.

It was all drivel, everything I was trying to pen. Yet, I knew I could probably still sell it, the regurgitated mess, but somehow, deep down, behind all the materiality instilled in me, the money was non-consequential.

It never really was all that important, even from the start. I wanted to write the next great "American novel". I had a good reason, an intrinsic reason, an admirable reason.

What was it again?

One night, I left my apartment and just started walking west on Bloor Street, it was 8 PM on a Monday and the sidewalks were packed to capacity, so much so that I could only maintain half speed, as I dodged and evaded arms and legs every few seconds. There was such energy to be felt, it was a moshpit.

I walked for about an hour, out to High Park and the little coffee shop a few blocks north of it I used to frequent called Tropic of Keele. The one where you had to call ahead and reserve a seat, while those who were less organized would line up out the door and around the block for a chance to get a bit of standing space inside. The one the famous American writers and occasionally actors would frequent whenever they were in town, while the local authors used it as a place to be seen as they indulged in the award winning pastries. The place where as a kid I often made the long trek from the Far East, notebook in hand, to scribble down beautiful nothings on tranquil Sunday afternoons while flirting with the cute hipsters, twice my age, drawn from the Downtown Westside.

"What are you writing?" They'd ask.

"Just a poem, about the change of seasons, I always find it really inspirational. Very moving." I'd reply, not believing it, but thinking it sounded deep.

They would light up, as if I'd just made some

groundbreaking revelation. "That's so true! I mean, I couldn't agree more. Can I read it?"

"Sorry. I mean, I'd love to show you but. It's just I don't show work to strangers." People love being told they can't have something. Once they are, they'll want it, even if they weren't all that interested to begin with.

"Well, we don't have to be strangers! I'm Josie." Or Amber, or Kelly, or Brittany, or Claire, or Robin, et cetera et cetera.

The coffee shop was still there, but it was dead. The only customers were an elderly couple who gave me a condescending glance as I ordered a black coffee and enjoyed it in silence. I was hungry but the only thing they served now was stale donuts. I took a look at the menu again and realized the prices for the drinks were about a fifth of what they used to be.

When I was a kid, there had been a nice little par-kette across the street, where year round people gathered to jam on their guitars. I used to be able to lock eyes with them from inside the coffee shop, I'd smile and they'd wave me over, I couldn't play a chord, but there was a comradery there, creative minds alike. Now, in its place there was a condo, maybe a year old, advertising penthouses starting at ten million.

There were various differences between present tense and my cherished memories, but Toronto still appeared to possess all the elements necessary to spur creativity. And yet, some subtle yet crucial variable was missing from the equation and I was awful at math.

There was no doubt about it, *Ten Feet Down,* if actualized, was to be my Gatsby. It probably would sell the fewest of any of my works, but it would be the most critically acclaimed, the most celebrated, the one that would stay behind as a shrine after I was gone from this earth and that prospect alone was almost enough to fill the void. Though, not quite...

I needed to break it, smash right through the block which was drowning me in shame and eighty proofs before I completely lost my mind, but as I dove deeper and deeper into the subconscious which both thrilled and terrified me with equal frequency, I found only a hollow abyss, filled with clichés.

And then I got very thirsty.

There's a line, it's different for everyone. I usually know better than to cross it, but when you do, there's no going back.

That feeling. It's like being young and horny. It perks you up, makes all other things meaningless, irrelevant. Life itself becomes little more than a nuisance or a distraction in the way of the newfound single goal. You know you can't sleep without attaining it, nor could you smile or find any sense of contentment. At least with sex there's masturbation as a cheap but sufficient compromise, with this, there is no substitute, when you want it, you need it. So find it. It's why every real drinker keeps a bottle of something they hate, stashed as a first aid kit. Mine is usually Sambuca (can't stand black licorice). But I'd forgotten to pick up a replacement bottle...

It was after ten, the Beer Store was closed, the LCBO too. It was after two, the bars were shut down and I could no longer remember the location of the emergency rooms-the afterhours bars run in and around Chinatown. There was to be no sanctuary for me.

So I went to a twenty-four hour pharmacy, the purchase as awkward as my first condom run, ten years previous. Perhaps even more so.

"Good evening, sir." The girl behind the counter said to me with a big smile.

"Hey."

"Is that everything?" She asked, as she pointed to the one liter bottle of mouthwash I'd selected. I had checked the aisles for one of the old school brands and found one that was 27 percent.

"Yeah."

"Do you have our rewards card?"

"No." Let's just hurry it up. There were people standing behind me in line. No one buys this stuff after midnight for proper use. They knew, and she knew they knew. Why was she rubbing it in? What had I ever done to her?

"We have a special on the mint flavor. Two for one, actually. Would you like to grab another one?" She asked me, she really didn't get it, to her it was just about minty fresh breath, her innocence was endearing.

"No, it's okay."

"You sure? You save a toonie!" For Christ's sake, stop mocking me! The judgmental elderly couple behind me were growing impatient, I gave them a smile, but they just sneered back. Old people have always hated me.

Then a beat cop entered the pharmacy. He smiled

at everyone but seemed to fixate on me the longest. I tensed up. Hurry! Hurry! Hurry!

"No. It's okay." I replied to her.

She was cute, and interested in older, mystery men. I could have gotten her number, taken her out the next night, had passionate sex, maybe even forged a connection. But instead I entirely avoided eye contact. I didn't want her to see me like this: eyes bloodshot, head pounding, stomach trembling, staring at the bottle of mouthwash and beginning to salivate.

I rushed back home, as quickly as my feet would allow and tore the packaging off with the intensity of a hemophiliac trying to open a Band-Aid wrapper. It wasn't proper to use a shot or pint glass in this circumstance, so I sat down on my couch and took the stuff back in large swigs straight from the bottle.

It wasn't bad. The artificial mint flavor effortlessly concealed the alcohol, so it was easy going down, though the aftertaste was so overpowering that my eyes would water as I hacked after every swallow. Still, I managed to get through half the bottle. I was out fifteen minutes later convinced I'd enjoyed smooth Crème De Menthe.

CHAPTER THIRTEEN

THERE'S A PHOTO in a nice golden frame up on my mother's bedside table. Of me and my father, smiling, while roasting marshmallows on an open fire up in Muskoka. She keeps it there to fool herself into thinking that was the norm.

I still remember the circumstances which allowed that photo to be taken. Maybe it would be better if I just forgot.

My father had been interviewing for a cushy low level, low maintenance, reasonably well paying government job. Normally he'd go to these things completely hung over. But my mum had just had her hours cut and we were so tight on cash that he could barely afford his whiskey. So he proclaimed he wouldn't have a single drink during the two-week process. To the bewilderment of us all, he kept his word. Towards the end he offered to take us all camping up north. Nick and Matt declined. So we got a lot of one-on-one time in.

"You know, Sean, I don't say this enough, but, I'm really proud of you, with the way you're growing up.

Matthew and Nickolas are always getting themselves into trouble, but you're a really good kid, a really smart kid, you're gonna amount to something big one day." He said to me, sincerely, as we sat together in the middle of the woods on a summer's night, a few feet from a roaring campfire.

I didn't know how to take it, so I just smiled and nodded.

"Here, you're holding it too far, let me show you," he had said affectionately, taking my stick and moving it a few inches closer to the flame. "That's how you get it nice and golden brown."

Sure enough he was right, it came out perfect.

He told me a joke, something derogatory about the English. I laughed.

Snap. Flash. Capture. The lie became immortal.

"So, you wanna be a writer huh? That's what your mother tells me."

"Yeah, I mean, that would be amazing." I didn't look at him, I felt stupid for saying it.

"Good lad! A lot of great Irishmen have made their names through it. What are you gonna write?"

"Poems, books, maybe movies?"

"Yeah? Your old man gonna get to be the first to read them?"

"Sure." I said, knowing I'd never let him read anything.

"It's a deal." He put his arm around me and gave me a kiss on the forehead.

He was a decent guy when he had the opportunity to properly dry out, a charming guy, hell even a nice guy. It was this side of him that had won over my mother when they were in high school. Back when he only drank two or three nights a week.

We saw this side of him maybe once or twice a year. On those biannual occasions where he got so sick that the very smell of booze would cause him to vomit. He would cool it for a few days and my mother would assure us he had finally done himself in. That he'd finally learned his lesson.

But as soon as he began to feel marginally better, as soon as he could bring it to his lips without hacking in turn, he would binge.

I never asked him why he started drinking, or more importantly, now that things had the potential to be pretty good, why he kept going. But then again, I rarely stop to ask myself. There is no easy answer, there is no logic to this puzzle, if there is, then the missing piece wasn't just removed from the box, it was thrown in a wood chipper and the fragments spread over the bottom of Lake Ontario…

Chapter Fourteen

I LOOKED AT MYSELF in the mirror for the first time in weeks and hated what I saw. My hair was thinning, my face was puffy and wrinkled, my gut was beginning to become noticeable through my shirt and my gum line was receding. I was twenty-seven but most people mistook me for thirty-five. I decided not to look in the mirror anymore.

It was a Sunday morning, so I went down to The Market-Kensington Market. It was hipster's paradise, the ammunition against every quip about Toronto being a boring, conservative city. A lot of starving writers procrastinated within its dive bars and vintage clothing shops. It was the kind of place where you'd get tossed out of a bar for being overdressed, so I threw on jeans and a t-shirt.

The area had cleaned itself up, but it was still cool. The chickens which had once run through its streets to avoid being beheaded had been replaced by some trendy new vegan restaurants. The dealers who had once sold their incredible grass right out in the open had been traded in for buskers, some playing music, some juggling flaming torches, other's breakdancing.

But some things hadn't changed. The burnt out car with no tires was still parked in the middle of the street, spurring a garden out of its engine block and covered in groovy illustrations right out of 1970's San Francisco. The second hand military outlet was still there, with its diverse selection of used bayonets, parachutes and gas masks. The hole in the wall pub, where I'd gotten my first ever hand job, from a wannabe photographer in the women's bathroom was still serving up pints of Pabst Blue Ribbon. And the indie art gallery where I'd once seen a grown man dancing around in a diaper as part of an exhibit was still promoting new shows. The mellow anthems of Jamaican reggae were still to be heard and the restrained hint of marijuana still glided through the air.

And there were still the specialty stores, the one selling cheese, the one selling hot sauce and the one selling nuts. The latter was notorious for being run by the friendliest old lady in the city, her and I used to banter all the time, she always claimed I'd be perfect for her daughter. So, after grabbing a spicy beef patty for the road – a former staple of my student diet, I stepped inside and took a whiff of the sedating odors of a hundred different varieties of nuts. They reeked of a childhood far removed.

"Hello handsome, what can I do for you?" She said, wearing a warm, inviting smile.

"Hey! Do you remember me?" I asked her with a smile of my own. She was in her fifties, but she was gorgeous: dark skin, tight breasts and thick curly black hair. I could only imagine how good her daughter must have looked.

"What?"

"I used to come in here every weekend. The kg of Brazilian walnuts, allergic to everything else. You remember? I was your favorite customer, few years back. Sean O'Connor, your future son in law?"

"My son in law, what are you talking about?" The smile vanished and the tension settled in.

"It's just a joke. You used to say I'd be perfect for your daughter? You even invited me over for dinner to meet her a few times. I was wondering if that offer was still on the table?" I explained.

"My daughter is married. Three years now. Very nice man with whom she have child. She is not for you." She crossed her arms and wore a hostile expression.

Come to think of it, maybe it was the cheese shop that had the friendliest old lady?

"Yeah. Sorry. I was just kidding." I added, trying to defuse the situation.

"Yes joke. Haha funny. You buy something now?"

The cheese shop for sure.

"Okay. A kg of Brazilian walnuts then, ones that haven't touched any of the other kinds."

She smirked, opened the tray and began to shovel nuts into a paper bag while I searched my wallet for a twenty.

And then the odors evaporated.

I looked up to see that the old lady had vanished.

"Hello?"

I quickly scanned the shop, I was alone.

The lights went out.

I stepped back outside.

The music ceased.

It was 11 am and the sky went completely black.

And then, I was in solitude. There was no one in the deserted market but myself and a couple of scurrying rats.

I checked my phone. The time was 1 am.

I'm dreaming…

You're not dreaming.

I started to shiver, when I exhaled, I saw my own breath. It was supposed to be twenty-five degrees today. I looked down on the ground and saw snow.

I'm dreaming.

You're wide awake for the first time in years.

And then I saw HER, across the street.

SHE was wearing a casual black dress underneath a dark brown leather jacket.

SHE rode black leather boots with three inch heels.

SHE was in a rush, moving as fast as HER footwear would allow while rubbing HER arms to stay warm.

SHE entered Nassau, one of the nicer bars in the area.

I crossed the street after HER.

When I got to Nassau's entrance, a bouncer stepped out in front of me. He was really tall, maybe 6'10, shaven head and serious bulk. "Sir, do you have an invitation?" He asked.

"An invitation to what?" I asked.

"Tonight's event is a private function. No invite, no entry."

"How do I get an invite?" I asked, reaching for my wallet. "How much?"

"I'm sorry sir, tickets are not for sale."

He stepped back inside the café and locked the door, leaving me stranded on the street.

I tried to peak in through the windows but they were tinted. They never used to be. I waited around for half an hour, but no one entered or left the bar.

As I left the market, the snow cleared and the night turned back to day, my phone showed the time as 11:05 am, I turned back and saw a crowd cheering on a busker riding a unicycle.

I'm dreaming, I told myself.

CHAPTER FIFTEEN

I WOKE UP TOO early.
I needed another three hours, maybe four to fully process the unusual mix of agave tequila, Polish vodka and Bermudian black rum from the night before. Apparently you aren't supposed to mix your liquor, it's one of those pesky little drinking "rules" I've never bothered to follow.

I spent the entire morning in the bathroom, my head resting over the bathtub (the toilet in that "luxury" apartment had become backed up). I puked up the remnants of the liquor as a light brown sludge. Followed by the water I hoped would help sober me up. But even when I became bone dry, my stomach kept compressing and I hacked up a few ounces of digestive acid, followed by a few droplets of blood. I wasn't sure whether those were from my throat or my stomach. I told myself I'd keep a real close eye on that.

* * *

Unlike music or acting, writing is a very lonely art. It's a professional requirement that you learn to isolate yourself, remove yourself from the positive though counterproductive influences of friends, family and lovers whenever the need so arises – and if you're good, it arises a lot. Like it or hate it, it's the only way you'll ever get anything done. That's why I always say, the ideal location for writing isn't L.A. it's not New York, it's not even Toronto, it's a prison solitary cell, where the only place to go, is inside your head. But since few of us are in a rush to get incarcerated (I drop the soap enough in my own shower) you just have to make do. You need to learn to create your own mental cells.

It's not like music, where you can effortlessly draw hordes of beautiful strangers to follow your every note, even if you are off key. There's always poetry as a means of getting immediate attention I suppose. But only a very keen intellect can appreciate that for what it really is and let's face it, the number of people completely seduced by a repetitive three chord progression will always exponentially outnumber those who can recite Eliot. Plus, I find the structure of it all far too restrictive. Writing should be free.

A lot of people think a writer's greatest fear is the day he or she wakes up and realizes that as a result of their self-induced segregation that they're now entirely alone. It's not. The greatest fear is the day you wake up and realize, none of that made any difference, you were alone from day one and that will never change.

Sure, you can have acquaintances: friends, lovers, family-have as many as you want. But sooner or later, you'll realize that no matter how much you talk and they listen, no matter how much you explain and they acknowledge, no matter how much you touch and they quiver, they will never understand you. If emotional connection can be modeled by sex (as most things in life can), then as a creative person, you'll spend your entire life wearing a very thick condom.

CHAPTER SIXTEEN

I PUT HIM ON speakerphone and ran the kitchen tap for effect, while silently smothering a bottle of rye in the background.

"Adam! You hear this man? This is me pouring my booze down the sink! I'm sorry man! Okay! I'm sorry for messing up your class! I'm gonna get dry, I promise! I need your help okay!" I said, dramatically. I wasn't sorry, but I wanted the chance to chat with him.

Janet was out for the evening with some girl-friends, so he agreed to meet up with me at Darla's, our old watering hole across from campus, home to the cheapest pitchers in the city, where to score some brownie points with teacher, I casually sipped on a Shirley Temple. The bartender couldn't even keep a straight face while preparing it. But you know what? I love this drink. I bet it would go great with an ounce of tequila.

"Adam, I was out of line. You're right, I took the low road up there and I'm sorry for that. Really sorry." I didn't believe the prepared drivel I was spouting, but he was far too good a friend not to lie too.

"Look, I'm sorry too man. I overreacted." He replied, cheerfully.

"So we're good?"

"Yeah man, we're good." We shook hands.

"Awesome."

He looked off into the distance. "I think about it a lot, Sean."

"Think about what?"

"How I'm somewhat responsible." I saw a small tear begin to form in his right duct.

"Responsible for what?"

"Your drinking."

"What? How?"

"The trip down to Mexico, High School, junior year. Remember?"

"What about it? It was an amazing time." And it had been. A bunch of us guys had gone down there for a week to an all-inclusive in Cancun. Our trip had coincided with American spring break, so the resort had been packed with hammered eighteen year old girls from the South and Midwest, all the right kinds of trouble. We'd bought a few green bracelets off them, the ones you need to flash at the bar in order to drink and then the world had been ours.

It was the first time I'd ever drank for the purpose of leaving the world behind and the whole process had been so effortless, so well lubricated. Three ounces of tequila and I was the sociable, happy, well-adjusted young man I would have been with a better father. Three more and I had the courage to approach any woman, no matter how beautiful. Another three and I was finally able to talk to my friends about things which actually mattered. And the next morning, I woke up feeling totally refreshed and energized, ready to do the whole thing over again.

I smiled, but he kept talking with the same somber tone ,"Before that you wouldn't touch the stuff. Told me you never would, that you didn't wanna end up like your brother or your old man. But I convinced you to indulge a bit. Have shots with us every night. I just wanted you to relax, have some fun. I didn't know you would get hooked so easy." He grabbed my hand and looked me square in the eyes. "I swear to God, Sean, if I had, I would never have let you go near it."

I laughed, remembering fooling around with a girl on one of the resort's pool tables after doing a few shots of tequila out of her pierced belly button, you don't even wanna know where she put the lime. "Man that was nothing, just a little youthful indulgence. You were right I did need to relax," I replied, suddenly longing for the past, to be sixteen and back on that trip again. Now-a-days the price for escape was borderline astronomical on both my wallet and my health. The mornings after were no longer forgiving.

"Man. I didn't start real drinking until I moved out west. It had nothing to do with you. It's that City of Fallen Angels that's to blame," I said. "The writer's block, it's just the worst feeling in the world, you know? I guess I kinda felt like I'd lost my purpose and the drinking's just been a way to distract myself from the possibility that maybe my resources are tapped, that I'm barren. But, that's impossible. I'll finish this puppy, get myself back in the game and get back to moderation. Don't worry about me, alright? I'll be fine." I was talking to him, but really I was convincing myself.

He let go of my hand and ran it roughly though his receding hairline.

"So I saw that girl again. The Ryerson one. Over in Kensi. SHE went into Nassau but the doorman wouldn't let me in. Said there was a private event or something."

His eyes bulged. "You went to Kensington?"

"Yeah."

"You told me you could never go there again."

"What? When the hell did I say that? I would never say that." I signaled to the waitress to bring me another Shirley. "I always loved that neighborhood and it's still pretty bitching."

He reached for his phone and sent a text. His phone vibrated from a message shortly after. He nodded at it in restrained recognition.

"Jan and I think that you should see a doctor, Sean," he said.

"What? Look at me. I'm drinking Shirleys here like a schoolgirl. I told you, I can kick this!" Or maybe it would taste better with white rum?

"Look, don't take this the wrong way. But I think you need to have your head checked."

"What! Why?" I laughed.

"You said you were clinically dead for a while." Two and a half minutes.

"Yeah, so what? What are you talking about man?"

He reached for this phone and I knocked it out of his hand. "Don't talk to her! You can talk to her when you go home for curfew. Talk to me! What the hell are you getting at?"

Suddenly, he totally lost his composure and just started screaming. It was the first time I'd ever seen anything like it, in fifteen years of friendship. "I think your memory is fucked Sean, okay? Completely fucked! I didn't know if it was from the shooting or from all the booze, I didn't wanna say anything at first, but you're really starting to scare me. I wish you could hear yourself speak man, you don't make any sense." The rest of the bar looked over at him and the commotion and it embarrassed him into calming down.

I had no idea what he was talking about. Though, I could feel it resonate for a second, chilling my marrow, causing it to ache, like a Canadian winter's night without gloves. "What is this?"

"Sean. You really don't remember, do you? The way you've been talking since coming home, you don't seem to remember anything. Hell you don't even remember what happened that night in Kensington?" He was beyond petrified, but in a selfless sense. I thought back to Kensi and the Sundays I'd spent there as a young man, but remembered nothing significant, aside from the previously mentioned hand job, that and scoring great weed in Bellevue Square. Speaking of which, I could really use either one of those things right about now.

"Why! What happened! I bought some bad hash! What! If it's so important, remind me!" I replied.

He took a deep breath and calmed down even further. "I'm sorry Sean. I can't do this with you. Okay? I can't do this."

"Do what?"

He finished his drink and got up from the table – dropping some cash and pushing his chair neatly back into place. "Look. I'm going to Hawaii tomorrow with Janet. We're gonna take a couple weeks and celebrate our ten year, at a really nice B&B right on the beach, maybe even try for a kid." He reached into his jacket and retrieved a business card. "His name is Ganton. He's a really good friend of Jan's. He's one of the best neurologists in the country. He's over at Yonge and Wellesley. Give him a call, tell him you know me, he'll pencil you in whenever you want." He tossed it onto the table, right in front of my juice.

"Oh come on man. Relax. I'm sorry I lost my cool. Just, have another drink with me." I insisted.

"No. Do it, please, for me, for yourself man. Promise me."

"Okay. Fine. I'll go."

"Promise me." He said, passionately.

"I promise."

I got up and hugged him that casual way North American men do. I was surprised how good it felt to be embraced. I didn't want him to let go.

After he left, I stuck around at the bar for a few hours, asking the tender to mix my Shirley first with rum, then with tequila and finally vodka, but somehow it never tasted as good as it did virgin.

* * *

After I left the bar, I tore the card in half and tossed it into an open sewer grate. Not because I didn't believe him, but rather because I was too afraid to find out if he was actually right.

I caught a glimpse of a bum and felt myself tense up. He was a sick old man, his frame skinny, his skin blistered and his clothes filthy and ragged. He was standing on the corner of Bloor and Spadina. He was screaming nonsensical gibberish fueled by the heroin his arms bore scars too. In his right hand a liter of bourbon, in his left, a cross.

As I passed by, he looked at me, dead in the eyes and spoke, hypnotically, we locked pupils and I couldn't break contact. *"Mea maxima culpa... mors mortis...ignoscere...circulus vitiosus"* He spoke, in perfect, crystal clear Latin as he robotically jerked his head from one side to the other.

I didn't know what it meant, I told myself I'd Google it when I got home but I never did.

The trance broke and he resumed spouting babble.

I dropped a twenty dollar bill at his bare feet with intention not to make eye contact again and then, feeling like there was a horror movie running in my head, made my way home, hoping I'd be able to find the remote, stop it, and put on a comedy instead.

PART III

October 2011

Toronto, Ontario

CHAPTER SEVENTEEN

WHEN IN DOUBT, start drinking. Fears, obligations, regrets, uncertainties, all find themselves trivialized by blessed intoxication. It's not the frat boys and cottage crowd that make it a multibillion dollar industry. Trust me. Their contributions are well exaggerated, mainly by the sexy, misogynist advertising of chicken shit beers. At the end of the day, it's the troubled souls desperate to temporarily evade a reoccurring problem who keep liquor executives in Ferraris.

Who says you ever have to come down? I'd take a prolonged buzz over a quick high any day of the week.

Most drinkers save their consumption for nighttime, they have to. If you wanna keep your nine to five you can't show up blasted. But for me, there was no boss to impress, no co-workers to pretend to be friends with, no client asses to kiss.

I'd kick things off in the morning with a few bottles of light blond beer because they were gentle on the gut. It would always ache when I woke up, but that was nothing a few Advils couldn't fix.

Around noon, after I'd had something to eat, I'd

move over to blended whiskey. I'd fill a coffee cup and sip on it while trying to write, the worse the writing got, the bigger the sips became. The writing was going nowhere. But that was okay, these blends went back oh so smooth.

When I started to get nauseous, I'd switch back to beer, stouts usually, they're full of iron and other valuable nutrients, everything a growing boy needs. Three or four of those and I'd feel like I'd just finished a turkey dinner.

With dinner, I'd consume a bottle or two of wine, generally something from Napa. I preferred reds, but I was willing to compromise if the pairing called for it.

Then with dessert, I'd crave something sweet so I'd pour a few ounces of Irish cream.

The nightcap was always single malt never less than eighteen years. That was to be consumed slowly, tenderly. I didn't just drink single malt, I made love to it.

And if after that, I couldn't sleep, I'd pop a Melatonin, chasing it with some 151.

Every week, the Melatonin got weaker, so I'd keep upping the dose. Eventually, I got up to eighty mg in a single dose (ten mg or less is considered "healthy"). With that kind of weight I'd be out in five minutes or less. But the dreams the pills brought on were so vivid and stimulating that I'd wake up the next morning completely burnt out, as if my subconscious had just done an Ironman.

Pretty soon, I'd need to find something stronger.

* * *

Adam was still in Hawaii and I was lonely.

There were new text messages from Steph and I felt so compelled to give them a read. But I didn't.

I thought about a few of the other girls, some in Los Angeles, some here in Toronto. I'd laugh or smile at particular memories, but couldn't remember to which woman they belonged. It was all a blur.

The only Toronto girl I still cared about was Patty. We'd dated casually for a few years during Uni. She'd always been fun, sincere and full of energy. Not a month went by where she didn't show up in one of my dreams, clothing optional.

I shot her an email and heard back within the hour.

We met up at a casual restaurant in Greektown for ouzo and souvlaki. She was there ten minutes early, I know because I was fifteen. She wore a concealing, prudish dress straight out of the 1910's. Her tired face void of makeup, showcasing an array of stress induced wrinkles. She was a good thirty pounds heavier, her once legendary figure, little more than a wet dream now. Her optimism long since shattered. I walked over to her table reluctantly.

"I can't believe it! Sean O'Connor! In the flesh!" She said with infinite enthusiasm.

"Patty?"

She grabbed me and gave me a hard hug that lasted three times longer than it should have. "It's so good to see you, hun!"

"Yeah, you too Patty." I hugged her back, but didn't feel the slightest bit aroused-the testosterone which had seared through my veins on the subway ride over now perspired from my forehead.

"You look great! Good to see you haven't lost that baby face!" She pinched my cheek.

We took a seat, across from one another, not bothering to eye the menus.

"Yeah. You look." She didn't wait for me to finish, afraid of what I might say.

"So tell me! How are things in L.A., Mr. Big Shot? Is it everything you always wanted it to be?" She asked me, her cheek resting on her hand, giving me her undivided attention.

"It's good. But it's nice to be back. I've always liked Toronto more." I replied.

"Really? Someone liking Toronto? Well that's a first!" She said to be funny, I didn't laugh.

The rest of Canada despises this city, own it up to jealousy. But no one hates Toronto more than Torontonians-it's the number one thing keeping us from being mentioned in the same sentence as New York or London. Most Torontonians seem to believe the city is a rundown shithole while the rest of the world is a divine paradise. I strongly encourage them to travel.

"Well what about you? I'm surprised you're still here. What's the deal? Are you killing it on King West or what?" She had a great voice, very unique and versatile. She sounded way sexier when she sang then when she spoke, looked way better when she danced then when she walked.

She lit up. "Oh my God! You remembered?"

"Of course. You were awesome! Tell me you're rocking the Royal, or the Wales?" Two of Toronto's largest theaters.

She rolled her eyes. "Oh! One can dream."

"Or did you cop out and become something silly? Like a doctor or a lawyer?" I said. She'd always been smart so either would have been well within her grasp.

"You always knew how to make me laugh."

She smiled, but it took a lot of effort. She ran her forearm over one of her eyes and left some residue on her cheek.

"Pat. Are you okay?"

"Sure. Just allergies."

"In October?"

"Can't get much past you, can I?"

I pulled my chair over to hers and put my arms around her to be comforting. "Do you wanna just bail on dinner, go somewhere to talk? I mean somewhere private?"

She nodded her head and the tears began to flow.

So I took her down to Woodbine Beach. Outside of summer, it was always abandoned after dark. We'd fooled around there on countless occasions. Dig around in the sand and you'll find at least ten of my condom wrappers, Trojan Magnums are my brand (no big deal).

"So, Sean. You have a special someone back in L.A.?" She asked me, I knew she wanted me to say no.

"Nah."

"What? Why not!? You must be a huge catch with the ladies, with that charming Canadian accent."

I laughed. "There hasn't been anyone special. Not for a long time." How long?

I don't remember.

"That's so sad Sean." And come to think of it, it

kinda was, as a kid I'd been convinced I'd be married by twenty-five.

I put my hands on her shoulders and began to lightly massage her. "Come on. You didn't wanna come all the way down here to talk about me, Pat. What's going on?"

She grasped my left hand, her own trembling. "I don't wanna burden you, Sean. You've got this amazing new life now."

"Pat, don't be like that, talk to me." I raised my hand from her shoulder to her pudgy cheek and stroked it gently. It made her cry once more.

"Well, everything just came together for you. You left and you made it. No one else here did. I went to New York and they just laughed me off the stage. Told me I wasn't fit for to be an extra in a middle school musical."

"Oh come on! Don't take a bunch of limp dicked casting directors seriously. They're all full of shit. You're an awesome actress Pat. I always loved the stuff you used to do over on the west side. You were good. You're still good."

"Sean." She was right, I had just left, I had just made it, I hadn't done much to help those left in the trenches. I thought about kissing her, even though she was no longer attractive, but I easily restrained myself, I was still pretty sober.

"Hell, I'll tell you what. Come back with me, to L.A. You can stay with me, enjoy the sights and all that touristy junk and I'll introduce you to some agents. They don't do much theater there, but you'd be great on the screen too. I can help you get in the game. It would be my pleasure."

Her tears increased. Her face was a waterpark with five slides. "I can't, Sean."

"Why? What are you settled down now?" It was supposed to be a joke. Then she lifted her hand and I saw the subtle white band of truth. Then I saw the scratches on her wrist, of various ages and depths. They weren't coordinated enough to be self-inflicted. They were defense wounds. My mother had always had them.

I took her wrist and inspected further "What the hell? What's up with your wrist?"

"Sean."

"Does he hit you?" I already knew the answer and the siege of anger struck me instantaneously. And then I realized why she was dressed so prude. I put my hand on the bottom of her dress and lifted it up, she didn't stop me. Her legs and torso looked even worse than her wrist. She was covered in scratches, cuts and bruises, some years old, some fresh, likely from that very day. A belt? A razor blade? A bottle? I couldn't tell. I dropped her dress back down. "Pat. What the fuck?"

"No. Sean, it's okay. Sometimes he drinks and it gets him angry. But, he only hits me when I deserve it. It's okay, really. I hit him too."

I took a step back and clenched both my fists. "Take me to him."

"Sean."

I heard myself begin to scream. 'No! This is fucking

bullshit! Take me to him! I'll bash his Goddamn head in!"

Her crying continued to exacerbate, her eyes turning red, her speech constantly interrupted. "Sean! Please. I can't stand to see you when you're angry, when you're drunk!"

"What?" I never drank around her, at least nothing more than responsible social drinking. As of now, I was perfectly sober, wasn't I? I was pretty sure I could sing the alphabet backwards on one foot upon request.

"He's the father of my children, Sean. Please don't hurt him." She begged. Children? When did this happen?

"You have kids?"

"Yeah. Two. Ben and Amy. They're my life." She reached into her purse and pulled out two wallet sized photos. Good looking toddlers that looked like their mother used to. I was pretty sure I could spot bruises on their faces.

"But I thought you didn't want kids early, you wanted to chase the dream?"

"Dreams don't exist for people like me, Sean." She said, rubbing her eyes and soaking her hands in the process.

"That's bullshit. If I can make it, so can you."

"I don't want to make it, Sean." She said with a bitter tenor.

She was still breathing, but she was no longer alive. This was the woman who in her teens claimed she would never want a place in the suburbs, but rather her own penthouse on Park Ave. Who wanted her name bolded, front and center in an Inquirer tabloid, because as she had put it, "if she was worthy of a sex scandal, then she was without question a *somebody*". She had been the one who had flat out refused to get exclusive with yours truly because she wanted to be able to pack up and go wherever the opportunity presented itself. The way I had, at twenty-two, when a pawned gold watch from my Confirmation had bought me a one way ticket to La La Land.

She quickly forced herself back together. "It was a mistake me coming here. I need to get home, I need to tuck the kids in, make sure they ate dinner. Don't take this the wrong way, Sean, but I don't think we should see each other again. She turned and began to walk away.

"Patty, please. I love you." The words came out on their own. I felt bad for saying them, even though, deep down, I knew I meant them.

She froze in place, in shock.

She turned and slapped me harshly across the face. "Don't you ever say that to me again, Sean, ever! Don't you ever lie to me again!"

"I'm not lying. I'm just saying what I feel. I mean, it's been a long time, but I swear, I never got over you." I moved in to hug her and she slapped me again, this time twice as hard. My jaw went numb.

"You don't love anybody else Sean. You can't."

"What the hell does that mean?"

"And I love Alan, Sean. I love him so much, he's everything to me and such a great provider and I would never want to do anything to risk losing him." She pulled out her wallet again so I could see her husband. It was a family photo and he wasn't smiling. Even my father had smiled for the portraits.

"Oh yeah, cause he sounds like a real winner. Christ. What the hell happened to you? The Patty I knew never would have let some deadbeat push her around. What the hell happened?"

"That was a different life Sean. A different life." She leaned in and gave me a quick kiss on the lips.

And then she was gone.

I stuck around on the sand for a few hours and thought back to the years her and I had dated. Memories came and went: sex over a tombstone in Mount Pleasant, skinny dipping in the lake after midnight, sloppy subway bar crawls and butchering classics at the Karaoke bars in Koreatown. Never any pressure, never any stress, never any expectation. Back when being able to drink a lot was considered impressive rather than problematic. It really was a different life.

Chapter Eighteen

I PUKED UP BLOOD this morning. Not vomit, not water, just blood, maybe two ounces worth.

It's my throat, it has to be, it aches so bad, I assured myself.

You really believe that?

I was scared. I needed a distraction. So I read Nate's novelette.

And to my complete shock, it was good. Way too good. Way better than anything I'd written at his age.

His story took place in and around the Scarborough Bluffs: a series of cliffs overlooking a rugged coastline and Lake Ontario. I'd gone there a lot back when I was a teenager.

The Bluffs were a tranquil place, devoid of the poverty, addiction and crime which defined much of the borough. It was the perfect place to brainstorm uninterrupted or even bring a notebook and free write. From Nate's story it seemed like it was a pretty important place for him as well.

I called him and set up a meeting at Beecher, the same café on Queen East where I had, at his age, gone to meet my mentors for feedback. It wasn't far from the beach, and its entire back wall was covered in windows. When they were open you could catch the cool breeze off the lake and if hammered enough, convince yourself you were sitting somewhere in Santa Monica.

He was there fifteen minutes early, oversized aviators to conceal a raging black eye.

"Where'd you get the shiner?" I asked him.

"Didn't think you'd notice." He removed them and placed them down on the table, next to his pint glass.

"We're writers. It's our job to notice." I took a drink of my pilsner and looked off onto the street, seeing a newscaster and a minor reality TV star walk by. This area was riddled with wannabes.

"Fell off my bike, hit a pothole." He said it pretty damn convincingly, writers make great liars. If I had asked for elaboration he could have written me a short story.

I laughed. "It's also our job to separate facts from bullshit. Come on, who am I gonna tell?"

"I get a lot of them. In Scarborough they give 'em out like frequent flyer miles."

"Well, well, a fellow vet of Scarlem. What part?"

"Malvern. You're from Scarborough?" He asked.

"West Hill, and if it makes you feel any better I got my ass kicked a lot growing up too."

"Really?"

"Sure. It's not an easy place to be creative or free spirited. But look, you gotta stay focused. You got a lot of talent. Your novelette was stellar, seriously."

"Really?"

"Yeah man, you should be really proud."

"Wow, thank you!"

"Keep writing Nate, keep writing. Good things will happen." I assured him.

"Too bad girls my age aren't exactly rushing to screw a wannabe writer." He replied. And that's always what it comes down to isn't it? The quest to get laid makes the world go round. When the earth is finally destroyed by a nuclear bomb, it will be because some insecure politician thought it would get him pussy.

I laughed again, quickly recounting a few of my proudest Southland "conquests".

One in particular came to mind. She was a twenty-one year old Swedish lingerie model. Despite being fit enough for a six pack, she had natural DD and a generous behind.

I had met her in a Starbucks in Beverly Hills, where she had been the one to approach me as I was pouring extra sugar in a Macchiato. She claimed she had seen me on a talk show, loved my books and wanted someone to help her write her blog. So I went back to her place and she went down on me while I edited her latest posting on her laptop. We shagged three times that day, her tits the bull's-eye.

There were a lot of stories like that-as soon as you got your mug on TV you became irresistible. They say the camera adds ten pounds, but it also takes your looks up ten notches, makes everything you say ten times more interesting, everything you've achieved ten times more impressive. I had always been a good looking guy, but I'd never had a woman come talk to me until I found success.

"They will, Nate. Once you make it. Out in Los Angeles, girls a thousand times hotter than the ones here are gonna be lining up for a shot with you. " I pointed down to the USB key. "I put my comments in red font, give them a read and let me know if you have any questions."

"Thanks, Mr. O'Connor, will do!"

"And keep me posted on your progress, alright? When you finish that first novel, look me up. I'll help you find a publisher."

"That would be amazing! Thank you so much!"

He was still young, still ambitious, still ripe with unmined resources. He was everything I still wanted to be.

And while he admired me, I envied him and wished for the life of me, that I could be on the other side of the table once again. But my heroes were long gone, either sold out or burnt out, me, I was both. Here in Toronto it was the same production, but I was the only returning cast member. Perhaps Steph had been right, maybe coming back here wasn't the answer, the thought began to cross my mind, yet I was far too stubborn to admit defeat and go back to L.A. empty handed.

So instead I went back to an old play pen, the section of Ossington Avenue between Dundas and Queen. Five years ago it had been my playground, my safe haven. Sure, the area had been a hub for crack-heads and their respective dealers, but, amongst the back alley deals and shattered vials in front of boarded up store fronts, it had been painfully genuine. It was a place where you could go as you were and find acceptance as such. Where gems of Mom and Pops outnumbered Starbucks by a generous margin. A place to escape the bullshit of the posh consumerist central city, if even for a few hours/pints. Plus the bars out there had never bothered to check ID.

Though I got there only to find it long since gentrified, now riddled with pick up artists and phony 905ers. But, I made due. In the back room of Sweat and Tears, perhaps the last true Ossy dive, I did my best to recreate the area of past through the assistance of my good friends: Jack, Jim and Jose. To the time when the spoiled, stuck up daddy's girls who wore skirts in minus thirty and the manicured suits who hunted them via liquid courage were held at bay, well east of Spadina by a combination of fear and disinterest. When the west side truly was a sanctuary for the creatively endowed, when the ability to spit poetic prose was in itself enough to get a phone number, or perhaps even to allow a woman to drop her guard entirely and reveal to you the inner workings of her complex and beautiful soul. Boy, those were the days.

I drank alone in a crowded room, my eyes to the ceiling, well above the heads of the joyous, carefree crowd sitting entirely in even numbers. They were laughing, dancing, thoughtlessly embracing while I gunned back shot after shit via Sean's Ark (two of each kind of liquor they had on the rack with only a one minute breather between hits). Shit after shot until I couldn't remember my middle name, among far more injurious things.

Who was SHE?

How do you know when you have cirrhosis?

What is the point of no return?

I caught the glance of a beautiful young blond. She was sitting with a pudgy unattractive friend who clearly wasn't able to hold her attention. She saw me and smiled, so I smiled back, it made her giggle. I waved her over, but she didn't budge, she just kept smiling and giggling. She whispered something in her friend's ear and she giggled too. This charade went on for a few more minutes, until the friend finally got up and came over to my table.

"Hey." She said with an incredibly deep voice.

"Hey."

"My friend wants to know, are you Aaron Sherbrooke?" Who?

"What?' I said.

"Is your name Aaron Sherbrooke?"

"No."

"Oh, okay." She turned and walked away, I didn't get a glance from either of them again. I Googled the name later, he was an executive working for MLSE, the company that owned most of Toronto's sports franchises. I didn't see the resemblance.

When my nearly bottomless wallet was finally empty and my mind too clouded to care about anything anymore, I stumbled home, carelessly flipping off each and every cab driver who tried to pick me up along the hour long trek back to The Annex. An hour long adventure which did not involve me getting mugged, beaten or shot. God, I love Toronto.

To all those living here who hate it and never shut the hell up about said hatred, put your money where your mouth is and get the fuck out. Move to Montreal,

Calgary, Saskatoon, Regina, Vancouver, Edmonton, Victoria, Halifax or Moose Jaw: the cities which according to you have completely extensive never delayed transit running 24/7, no crime, spotless sidewalks you could bend down and lick, plentiful jobs you won't need experience to get and people so friendly they'll hug and kiss you as soon as you leave the mansion you'll be able to buy for peanuts. Go on, leave, no one will miss you.

CHAPTER NINETEEN

IT CHEERED ME up when I was too nauseous to drink further-the shameless self-indulgence, the kind I'd found in exhausting excess over on the West Coast, but here was oh so deprived of. So I went over to The Arts District on the gentrified Queen West and dicked around in the trendy bookstores, the kind where people actually broke bindings rather than coffee lids and hoped to be noticed, recognized, by someone looking for an autograph, or even better, a set of digits.

Posing like a runway model around a number of different establishments, subtly but still aggressively enough to actively standout. I wanted them to come to me, to compliment or even intelligently criticize me. I wanted to become someone's Facebook status or even the foundation of one of an unexciting individual's embellished tall-tales.

Though this proved too much too ask, guess everyone was at work, that's the problem with being a self-run millionaire, for you everyday is a Sunday.

So instead, within the soothing confines of a

deserted second hand bookstore, I settled for shuffling through the dusty racks in pursuit of an early edition of one of my novels. There's something strangely soothing about buying your own books, I've got a dozen copies of each of the three on my shelves back in La La Land.

They had a vintage one-a first edition of *Dead Heart*. I opened the cover in search of an exact date, only to find an inscription in my messy, barely legible handwriting. I never left inscriptions.

To Lauren.

In five years this meaningless array of words and postulations will finally buy you your Fifth Avenue engagement ring.

Sean XoXo

Who the hell is Lauren?

"Excuse me. Do you remember who gave you this book?" I asked the kid behind the counter. He was in his early twenties, dressed in vintage: an army jacket and glasses with no frames. He reeked of pot.

"Let me see." He said, scanning the book and checking his computer. "Sorry man, there's nothing on it, must have come in before we setup our inventory system."

"When was that?"

"Two, three years back?"

"This book has been here three years?" In L.A. my books flipped over weekly, even used.

"I would say so." He inspected it further. "But if you want my advice, try something else. O'Connor's stuff is pretty pretentious." I'd gotten hundreds of bad reviews, but no one had ever called me that.

"How's that?"

"The guy thinks he's a founding member of The Lost Generation or The Beat Movement or something. He goes on all these dramatic rants, talking down to the reader like he knows so much more than them, it's a pain in the ass." What a prick. What had he ever written?

He handed the book back to me and I took a look at the author's photo on the last page. It was twenty-three year old me. My hair was thicker, my build was slimmer and my face was glowing with promise and optimism. Then I saw the price tag: 99 cents. I tripled checked it.

"This is 99 cents?" I asked the kid.

He took it back from me and examined it. "Yeah man, looks like it. We drop the prices on the books that don't sell." A chocolate bar was supposed to be 99 cents, something which was mass produced by thoughtless machines and meant for one time thirty second consumption. This had taken me a year to write.

"This is bloody sacrilege." I said to him.

He laughed. I didn't.

I gave him a loonie, went home, tore out the first page with the inscription for further inspection, signed my John Hancock on the second and then popped it up on Ebay where within three hours it sold for a cool $5000 to a grad student in Los Angeles. I didn't do it because I wanted the cash, I just needed to once again, feel a sense of self worth.

And as I was finally falling asleep, thanks to 100 mg of melatonin, my phone vibrated uncontrollably.

Text message. Unknown Number: *I Love You Sean. Please don't shut me out. We need to talk. I'll be waiting for you, as long as I can...Lauren XoXo*

I tried to text back but the send failed.

CHAPTER TWENTY

I WAS AGAINST THE Los Angeles traffic on a one way street up a San Francisco hill in the San Diego heat. I needed to stop pushing, take a step back-hit the restart button.

I'd drink every last drop in the apartment: eliminate all of the distractions, the temptations, enjoy tonight and then starting tomorrow force myself to stay away from the liquor stores and the overpriced adult daycares until I was done every last daunting page. This would be the last time, the last night defined by orgasms of irresponsibility. I had to make it count. This had to be the best night ever.

I hadn't made a liquor run in over a week so all I had left was an assortment of scraps, a few ounces here and there. I gathered everything in one central location, nearly empty bottles of vodka, rum, gin, tequila, good scotch, filthy rye and the emergency Sambuca. I had to finish it all in one sitting.

I fired up my laptop and watched *Heartless*, taking a drink every time the film took a creative liberty with

Dead Heart. By the fifty-five minute mark, every bottle was empty-I figured about twenty-three ounces.

For ten minutes I was euphoric. Laying there on the living room floor every part of me felt massaged by invisible hands and every worry took its recess. I felt horny, so I fired on a porno spoof of *Heartless* (which actually stuck closer to my novel than the Hollywood film) and had an incredible orgasm. I saw a crack on the ceiling and I laughed at it, so long and so hard that my abs ached as though I'd just done a thousand sit-ups. I pulled out my phone and drunk-texted a few people, telling each and every one of them that they were awesome and that I loved them. Steph was one of them. She texted me back but I didn't read her message.

I laid on my bed. I'd need ten hours. I could start writing first thing in the morning.

I got comfortable and closed my eyes.

You're fucked.

And suddenly I was in a barrel being tossed over Niagara Falls. Spinning, around and around, over and over, falling so fast I'd die on impact. I opened my eyes and the whole room was revolving, a giant washing machine. The floor became the ceiling, the ceiling became the floor, and then I was lying on that humorous crack.

And then the room rotated and I was tossed from the ceiling back to the floor, my head smashing against the wall in the process.

I instinctively assumed the fetal position.

And as I sweat, shivered and convulsed, from the earthquake and enduring aftershocks, as I coughed,

belched and clenched my chest tight to try and miti-
gate the incredible radiating pain, to convince myself
I wasn't going to have a heart attack, as I held my
breath to try and keep it all down, the increasing nausea at bay, I could, for a few dozen seconds, un-erase
an abstract painting of HER. SHE was sitting there
across from me, in that very living room, cross-legged
on the same scruffy couch. That girl. HER long dark
hair flowed overtop an I Love T.O. T-shirt SHE'D
picked up five for $3 from a vendor in Chinatown.
Lauren, yeah that was HER name, Lauren.

SHE was blowing kisses at a younger, healthier
me, a sober me, who sat there on the floor alongside
HER. He was completely composed and coherent,
reading to HER my first finished manuscript for *Dead
Heart*, as SHE playfully pointed out each and every
grammatical error, in the kindest, gentlest tone.

And then, just as I began to smile, just as the igni-
tion sparked, just as the loneliness retreated into the
often ignored index, SHE pulled back, and I had to
watch HER fade away, pixel by pixel, waving good-
bye, without intent to return. And I reached out for
HER, desperate for an affection I could remember
only in the pit of my stomach: a true affection, one
free from the cold calculating mantra which defined
all those in memory. One where there was more to
love than simply desperation, financial security or
familiarity.

Though when I reached what little was left of
HER, I was whipped back to reality. I was lying there
alone, on the eroded, ant covered carpet in an ocean
of my own vomit. My throat was eroding rapidly

from the harsh acid, my head was throbbing to a 6/8 beat, my hands were bleeding uncontrollably from the shards of a mutilated bottle of vodka.

I'll never drink again…

PART IV

November 2011

Toronto, Ontario

Chapter Twenty-One

NATE CALLED ME a few weeks after our meeting to run some ideas for a novel by me. At the time I was sitting in front of an empty screen on my laptop, down to the last two ounces of a Texas mickey of rye, I needed a break.

He wanted to write a book about a bank robbery orchestrated entirely online by a crack team of hackers. The premise didn't interest me in the slightest but I was glad to see him working on a project.

He took everything I said as gospel so I starting meeting up with him on a weekly basis. We'd pound beers in my apartment and come up with ideas for his novel, jotting them down on a chalkboard I'd found in the alley behind my apartment.

For the first six-pack, we'd stay on track. With the second, we'd both start to open up.

We had a lot in common. Obviously the Scarborough and writing connections, but on top of that, we'd both had psychopaths for fathers. If anything, his was worse.

Nate was fourteen when he witnessed his drunken

father beat his mother into critical condition, while he watched from the upstairs banister, wanting to help, but too afraid to move. They'd just lost a son and she'd failed to bring into this cruel world a replacement.

"You fucking bitch! You did this on purpose! Just to humiliate me, didn't you?" She had only been home from the hospital a few minutes, he hadn't bothered to go with her, the Leafs were playing. So she bore the bad news alone. Still, as soon as he saw her walk through the door empty handed, he knew.

She took his arm and dropped to her knees, begging. "No! No John. I swear. I swear, I did my best. The doctors all say I'm too old. But I did my best!"

He raised his pitch into a mocking tone. "Your best? Aw, you did you bestest? Did you really?"

"I swear! I'm so sorry John!"

"Your best? Then your best isn't good enough you fucking whore!"

His brass knuckles, engraved with his initials, a memento from his childhood in Glasgow did the rest of the talking, forcing imprints into her skull.

When her legs had stopped flailing, his father took Nate aside for a one-to-one. "I know you watched, but it's okay. You're gonna be a man and keep quiet about this aren't ya? If they ask, you're gonna tell 'em a dirty nigger broke in and beat her up. I don't have to deal with you too, do I?" He clenched the bloody iron for effect.

"No sir. I'll tell them, dirty black guy." Nate replied, doing his best to maintain eye contact, the way he always demanded.

She came back from her next trip to the hospital

noticeably different. Her speech was slower, her movements uncoordinated, her memory constantly betraying her. Still, he kept his mouth shut. Until, he saw him break a bottle over her head for getting in the way of the TV during a re-run of some eighties game show.

His father saw one year in prison, before being released on early parole for good behavior, the "experts" claimed he would be returning to the family completely rehabilitated.

As soon as he walked through the door, his breath reeking of bourbon, he took Nate by the arm and tossed him into the laundry room, slamming the door behind them. He looked his son dead in the eye and uttered calm words with the most menacing expression he'd ever exhibited "I know what you did, Nate. You think I'm stupid, but I'm not. I've had a lot of time to think about how you betrayed me and what I'm gonna do about it. You won't know when it's going to hit you, or how. But, you're gonna pay for this you little shit. You can count on it." He gave his son a pat on the back and a wink as he left for the washroom, finding it locked, he smashed his fists on the door.

"I gotta piss! Get the fuck out!" He screamed.

"Give me two minutes John, please" His wife had replied from inside.

"I'll give you five fucking seconds to open this door, woman!" He kept banging his hands, one particularly hard blow leaving an indent the size of a baseball in the cheaply made door. "Christ! Look what you made me do!"

"John! I'm on the toilet, give me a minute."

"I don't have a Goddamn minute!" He screamed

back, kicking the door, breaking it off its hinges. He grabbed his wife off the toilet by her neck and threw her crudely to the hallway hardwood floor, knocking out two of her front teeth in the process.

"Stupid fucking bitch, when I tell you to do something, you better damn well do it!" he kicked her in the face and broke her nose. He'd eventually scream at her to clean up the blood she'd expelled from the blow and to have the door fixed by morning.

Once his bladder was empty, he went promptly to the reclining chair in front of the TV and polished off a mickey of rum in five minutes flat. In that year, he hadn't missed a step-apparently he'd been scoring plenty of moonshine on the inside.

And as promised, the payback did come, six weeks later. It was 3 am and Nate awoke in a cold sweat to find his hands bound in thick rope to his bedframe and his mouth covered in duct tape. The lights were off, but he could make out the figure standing beside his bed, his father, one arm concealed behind his back, the other smoking a cigarette.

"You know what happens to white guys like us in the joint, Nate? The niggers fucking come at us, right out the gate, try and break us, like we were the ones who personally fucking enslaved them. My first day a spade tries to take my lunch in the cafeteria. I know he's trying to punk me, so I knock the bastard out with my steel lunch tray. A Scot-hating hack sees it go down so they throw me in the hole. Small little box with no lights or windows, leave you in there to roll around in your own shit for a week," he said, letting out a puff of smoke into his son's face. "My first night out I wake up in the middle of the night, tied up just like you. They were standing over me, the fucker I hit and a few of his guys, they're telling me I'm gonna pay, and I did, I sure as hell did," his father said, as he put the cigarette out on his forearm without flinching.

He turned on the bedside lamp and pulled up his shirt revealing his chest. The thick hair which had once occupied it was gone and in its place was a giant bulging scar the size of a shoe, some of it blood red, the rest pale white.

He dropped his shirt back down. "I got a little surprise for you, Nate, same one they had for me." He pulled the hand from around his back – in it was a clothing iron. It had been on for a while and it was steaming hot. Nate could hear it sizzle.

He pressed it firmly into the center of Nate's chest, the initial shock brought more adrenaline than it did pain, but as his father kept it there, smiling at his son's petrified pupils, the pain finally caught up, spreading across his entire torso, as the smell of burning flesh increased in potency. Nate screamed, but behind the tape, they were nothing more than helpless murmurs, drowned out by his father's laughs.

He kept it there, pressed into Nate's sternum, until his son lost consciousness.

He gave his son a smack across the face to revive him. "Hey! Shithead! Wake up!"

He pulled the iron away, bringing some chunks of skin along with it.

Nate took a look down at his chest, at the lumps of dead skin and exposed seared flesh and at the blotches of blood. The iron had cauterized well.

His father turned the iron off and tossed it to the floor. He reached into his back pocket and brought out a hunting knife which he placed against his son's throat.

"You know what they do to snitches in the joint, Nate?" He moved the knife against Nate's skin delicately. "They carve 'em up like turkeys. You ever rat on me again and I'll show you exactly how it's done." He slid the knife down Nate's stomach, towards his groin. "I'll fucking cut you from your cock to your throat. But you won't make me have to do that, will you?"

Nate nodded his head furiously.

"Of course not, no son of mine would ever be that fucking stupid."

And he didn't snitch again.

* * *

Over the next six months, the bruises and the bottles stacked up side by side, as if they were in competition. But with both of these entities in ever growing abundance, the formula was simply not sustainable. Something had to give, either the liver or the skulls. Fortunately for Nate, on his sixteenth birthday, it was the former. The addict, unable to shake the stomach pain through even the harshest pill fled to Vegas, leaving only a note stained with blotches of black rum, to go out in one final bang: with a sixty of whiskey, five hookers and an eight ball of coke, along with his family's life savings.

Family,
I am sick of you. Holding me back, wasting my fucking

time with all your whining and bullshit. So I am leaving you for a wonderful place called Vegas. Go fuck yourselves.

The police found him a week later, in Downtown Vegas, naked, sprawled out in a flea bag motel's roach ridden bathtub. Alcohol poisoning, they said.

CHAPTER TWENTY-TWO

I WAS WALKING EAST on Dundas when I caught it out of the corner of my eye: *Anything for a Dollar*, screening one night only at The Republic art house theater. It was advertised as including a very special Q & A session with the director Quinn Ross – a wannabe auteur, all around talentless hack. I couldn't resist another stab at him. The last time had been at a boutique theater in the L.A. Art's District, where I'd gotten the tool booed off stage after only thirty seconds of impromptu heckling. The show was sold-out, so I gave a guy outside $100 for his $20 ticket.

The source material for Ross's big budget blockbuster had been my second novel, a prize of a work I'd written after a few encounters with the working girls of Parliament Street. It was a brutal book, cynical and overly critical, relentless in its presentation of one central theme: there is a price for one's dignity and it's cheap. The protagonist, a rich girl from Rosedale, learns this the hard way, when after being kicked out of Yale for drug possession and being disowned by her disgraced family, is forced to sell herself around the Regent Park housing projects in order to survive. In the end, under the influence of her charming pimp and a pool of liquid assets she chooses to remain on the street even after being offered a second chance at a normal life, only to be murdered by a violent client, one of her father's wealthy friends no less.

The film used the title and nothing more.

It was a rehash of a nineties chick flick which was in itself a rehash of a seventies comedy, itself a rehash of a forties classic. The setting was changed to Upper East Side Manhattan, and the sex and violence were removed to attain a PG-13 rating.

The plot revolved around a wealthy young social-ite played by Tag Lambert, (a good looking third generation Hollywood rich kid casted solely on his flawless reading of the virtue of nepotism) giving a beautiful young prostitute a thousand dollars a day to pretend be his girlfriend in order to ignite jealousy in his estranged wife in an effort to win her back. Only to discover in the final ten minutes that he's falling in love with his underclass companion. Sound familiar? It should.

It was Classical Hollywood Cinema at its very worst, with nothing new to bring to the table. Though that didn't stop it from bringing in 200 million and an influx of critical acclaim, especially once Lambert was murdered while on vacation in Mexico at only twenty-four. The role was hailed his finest performance and the film was labeled a bold brilliant masterpiece. If you thirst for meaning hard enough, you can see Van Gogh in drywall.

Your book is your child. You spend as much of your

time with it as you can afford. You love it unconditionally, watch it grow up and become a finished product that reeks of you, your good sides and your bad. You swear to promote it, protect it through fire and ice. You only want the best for it and in turn, the best comes to you. So when someone alters it, for the worse no less, it's only natural for you to lash out. Not to mention, though I'd never tell my other "kids" *Anything for a Dollar* was the favorite.

Quinn Ross took front and center as soon as the credits rolled, dressed in an Armani suit threaded with complete and total confidence. For as long as he'd been around the L.A. scene, he was a pretty young guy, thirty-three, though he'd already had a hair transplant and a face-lift. He wasn't an American, but he refused to tell anyone where he had come from. He spoke with a really over the top Cali drawl and had openly admitted to hating foreign films. He went to The Oscars every year, but left as soon as the red carpet interviews had concluded.

"Thank you. Thank you. Thank you! You know. First off I just need to say, I feel truly blessed to be attached to such an incredible film. It's an experience I can't even put into words to envision and actualize a project as ambitious as this and then to see it win over crowds and critics alike. I only wish Tag could be here today to celebrate with me." He monologued, trying to sound dramatic, although it was clear he was just reciting something utterly soulless that he'd memorized and spoken a hundred times before.

They ate it up like starving mutts, the girls in the

front row blushing uncontrollably at his classless arrogance.

The further they got from California, the more powerful these guys became. The further they got from California, the most likely the fable was still alive and well. He spoke on and on for a good twenty minutes about how he felt the movie had saved American cinema and how it was difficult for him to go anywhere in the world without being recognized for it. Then finally, after finishing his fifth bottle of water and taking a good glance at himself in a nearby mirror he went on to the Q + A.

"So I think it's only fair that I let you echo the voices of the picture and open it up to some questions."

A sea of anxious hands.

"Yeah, you. The pretty girl in the red top." He pointed to a girl in the second row, she was stunning, why didn't girls this hot come to my Q + A's?

"Mr. Ross?"

"Yeah, sweetie?"

She blushed at the title. "How did you come up with the story? I mean, like, it's so honest and bold."

He took a deep breath and pretended to think. "Oh well, you know. I can't say exactly. I find inspiration in oh so many things. Maybe my time living in Hollywood, during the nineties, when things weren't as glossy there as they are today."

"What do you mean?" She was clueless.

"Well darling, Tinsel Town has had its issues believe it or not. It's not all film premiers and award ceremonies."

"Oh, I didn't know that." She said apologetically.

"Yeah sweetie, I'm not gonna lie, I've braved some pretty serious drama on my journey to success. Enough for a movie in itself."

"Wasn't it supposed to be based on a book?" I called out from the back of the theater before he was able to masturbate any longer. He'd never lived in Hollywood, since arriving in California he'd never left Beverly Hills without a limo and armed guards.

"Well, it is, very loosely." He caught my torrid glance and half his poise dissipated into the smug air. Another shark from La La Land, there was only enough room in the cinema for one of our egos.

I stood up and took position in the aisle. "Yeah, loosely is the key word, isn't it? Tell me, did you even read it?" I crossed my arms and waited to see what he could come up with.

"I read all I needed to." He replied in a weak tone. He was already on edge, and I hadn't even gotten started.

"So what? The jacket? The Coles notes? Maybe if you had broke the binding you wouldn't of had to knockoff a nineties chick flick, scene for scene." Usually this was when the cavalry arrived.

The crowd erupted into a concert of defensive boos. It restored Ross's dignity and he smiled once again.

"Sir. We're trying to have a productive discussion about the film. Can I kindly ask you to, get the fuck out?" he said.

They laughed profoundly, with shock value, as if it was the first time they'd ever heard the word.

"Ladies and gentlemen say hello to Sean O'Connor! " He pointed to me and gave a thumbs down sign.

I was hoping for support, or at worst disinterest, I got neither.

"The book was bloody drivel!" One of them shouted out. "Most overrated Canadian novel of the decade!"

"And what? The movie was better? It's a stupid rom-com!" I retorted fiercely. When someone puts down your child, you stand up for them.

"At least the movie didn't hide its influences. You didn't give credit for anything you stole!" Another yelled out.

"I stole? What the hell did I steal? It's an original novel."

"Hardly! You stole it from *Deja Mort*!" What?

"*Deja Mort*? What the hell is *Deja Mort*?"

"It's a French novelette, written by Pierre Blanc. Exact same story, twenty years before you!" He replied, as he stood up and pressed his scrawny, vintage covered body out in confrontation.

"Ok first, I've never even heard of that, so no I didn't steal from it, and second, I hate to burst your bubble, but everything's been done, there are no new ideas left, it's all about how you package them. Besides how many books have you sold, big shot? What gives you the right to criticize me?"

He was out of steam and sat back down, but within seconds someone else stood to take his place.

"Why are you even here? Isn't there a gala in Hollywood you should be at?" Sarcastic oohs and awes from the crowd.

"What?"

And then another. "Face it, you're just another Canadian sellout, got big and forgot all about your home. You don't belong here. This theater is for real artists."

I cracked up. "Excuse me? Forgot? Every one of my books is set in Canada. And that hack onstage is not a real artist! You can't bash me if you aren't gonna bash him. I mean, come on – he's directing the new *Teenage Vampire* movie!"

"The movie version was better! Tag Lambert was amazing!" Another anonymous hater.

It was like talking to a group of four year olds, a group of four year olds ripe with an array of learning disorders. They didn't want to reason or constructively argue, their minds were made up and decidedly inflexible.

When I left, they sang me out.

It hurt at first. This clique used to love me. But you know what? Fuck 'em. Who needs 'em?

When you're poor, they claim they're your best friend and sure they'll come in hoards to the "pay what you can" coffee house readings, filling the tip jar with lint and the room with their arrogance. They'll take everything from you: escapist entertainment, mental stimulation, free food, whatever they can get their hands on. But at the end of the show, don't except them to help pay your rent.

It's not that they're cheap-it's that it's not in their best interests. They want you poor, they want you gritty. They want you authentic, so that they can add you to their Facebook favorites list to up their social status through artistic obscurity. But those things don't put food on your table.

Then you find some success-make enough to rival their trust funds.

Then you're comfortable enough to devote yourself entirely to your craft.

Then to them, you're a sellout, a traitor.

What a crock of shit.

Chapter Twenty-Three

MY PHONE RANG – unknown number. Usually I wait for the voicemail, always been more of a texter. But this time, out of pent up curiosity, I answered it on the first ring.

"Hello? Is this Mr. O'Connor?" An older woman's dry voice, not exactly what I was hoping for.

"Yeah? Who's this?"

"This is Jackie Orientel, I'm with St. James Hospital. Do you know a Nathan Rode?"

"Yeah? Sure. What's going on?"

"Can you please come down? As soon as possible?" My chest clamped up and I began to feel nauseous, even though I was totally sober.

"What's going on? Is he alright?" I asked. My voice frantic, my pace rushed.

"Please sir. Can you please come down? I'm not at liberty to discuss his condition over the phone."

I dressed half-heartedly, the majority of my dress shirt buttons mismatched, and hustled down University Ave, stricken with worry for a boy I hardly knew and yet somehow, felt a strong sense of duty to.

I got to the ER and checked in. Forty-five minutes later, I was called and placed in a little room for another thirty. There, I anxiously waited amidst the bitter screams and desperate cries ringing from the adjacent rooms, including a boy around Nate's age that was dying from a cocaine overdose. Apparently his friends had thrown him at the steps of the hospital from a moving car.

Finally someone bothered to show up. "Mr. O'Connor?" He was a fatigued, indifferent doctor, eager to finish up "work" and get home to his family. I didn't hold it against him. In that line of work, much like writing, desensitization was a professional necessity.

"Is he alright?" I asked.

"He's in the OR."

"What happened?"

"I'm afraid I can't disclose that to anyone other than his kin. We found your number in his cell phone. We were hoping you could help us get in touch with his mother? We've tried her home and work number, haven't been able to reach her."

"I don't know her."

"So you have no idea?"

"No. Come on man, what happened?"

He looked around to make sure there was no one in listening proximity. "He consumed twenty ounces of vodka with some over the counter sleeping pills. Suicide attempt we expect." It was some pretty heavy shit but the guy didn't care. He kept speaking with the same monotone voice, occasionally pausing to yawn.

"Christ. Is he going to be okay?"

He looked off at a sexy young nurse and gave her a wink and a smile. She blushed and then mouthed the words: "Call me".

He turned back to me, a smile on his face and a bulge in his pants. "We've got him intubated and under observation, but yes, he should be fine, he's very lucky."

"When can he go home?"

"We wanna run some more tests. Frankly I'd like to see him here a few more days."

"Okay, you have my number."

This is your fault.

Chapter Twenty-Four

I T WAS MY mother's birthday. I wanted to head to Montreal and surprise her but figured I'd better stick around Toronto in case Nate needed any help.

She and I have never been particularly close, not because we don't get along, but I suppose rather because I've always fancied myself too independent to appreciate mothering. I think she always took that the wrong way.

Unfortunately it's too late to mend things. Her mind is all screwed up. I don't know the medical term for it, I don't remember it anyhow, but she's all over the place. With her, past, present and future are all rolled into one. Half the time she thinks I'm still ten and questions whether or not I've done my homework or she thinks I'm forty and asks about her grandkids, sometimes she doesn't know who the hell I am at all. I thought about putting her in a home but couldn't bring myself too, so instead she lives in a two bedroom condo I bought her in Quebec. It's a five minute drive from her older brother Patrick, the only other family she has outside Ireland. Patrick's a drinker but he's the happiest drunk I know, she's well taken care of.

I called her in the morning but she didn't answer. I tried again at noon and once more in the late afternoon. I finally reached her after dinner.

"Hey Ma! I've been trying to reach you all day! Where you been?"

"Oh hi, honey!" She sounded really happy, really energetic, half her age. "I've just been here."

"Well, I think your phone might be messed up then. You didn't hear it ring?"

"It's working fine. Matthew's just been using it so much, that's all."

"Matthew?" Some days with her were better than others, today was a God awful one indeed.

"Yeah! You know the way your brother is! Him and all the girls he sees, they're always calling, I keep telling him to just use his cell phone, but he's so stubborn! Guess you get it from him."

I took a deep breath and clenched my forehead. "Mum. Mum. Matt's dead." I said to her, as gently as I could. Every time I reminded her, it was like breaking the news for the first time. I didn't know how many more times I could do it.

"What!" She sounded shocked. As shocked as the day the police had visited our house.

"You haven't been taking your medication have you?" The meds couldn't cure her, but they kept her more grounded, though every once in a while, she forgot. It was a vicious cycle, once she forgot to take them, she forgot she needed to take them, then she forgot she even had a problem. Maybe she did need to be in a home.

"What do you mean he's dead? We just had dinner together, my ravioli, with the sauce you love so much! When are you coming home anyway?" My guess, to her, I was sixteen again.

"Mum. Matt's been dead a long time. I want you to go to the cabinet and take your medication, okay? It's in a little orange bottle with your name on it, can you do that right now for me, please?" It never got easier-talking to her when she was this confused was the only thing that could still make me cry. I used to be a lot more emotional, shamelessly exaggerated in either extreme. Now I felt increasingly subdued. I don't fear hatred or suffering or death, but indifference on the other hand is utterly terrifying.

Young people always take their parents for granted. In North America, to come to despise them is as much a right of passage as losing your virginity. The scariest day of your life is the one where you and them switch roles and you take the burden of experience and responsibility off their aging backs. And then you come to realize, finally comprehend, the logic behind every restriction they ever imposed. Because as an adult you're your own parent, imposing your own self-restrictions. Or so you try...

I would have given anything to be sixteen again, able to go to her for advice, able to dump all my problems at her feet and feel completely content that she would be able to solve them for me.

Now-a-days if I even wanted someone to listen it came at a cost of $300 an hour. I saw a shrink in L.A.

for a while, he spent most of our sessions ogling his secretary, a sexy twenty-one year old Latina-through a huge window he had facing his reception area. All while giving me cheap grins and then the same three words of advice, over and over again "Go to Rehab, Go to Rehab, Go to Rehab" what a joke.

"What medication? I don't have a headache. You really shouldn't take pills when you don't need them Sean, they aren't good for you."

"Mum."

"Honey, will Lauren be joining you for dinner Sunday?" I stopped dead in my tracks.

"What?"

"Lauren. Is she coming?"

It wasn't fair, but I had to. "Yeah, SHE might be. Is that okay with you?"

"Oh yes! I just love her to pieces dear! She's a real keeper! Trust your mother for once. Don't let this one go!"

"Did I tell you SHE'S going to Ryerson? I told you what SHE'S going to study right?" A good leading question – might help jog my own memory a little.

"Ryerson? I thought she was planning to go to that school up in that awful Jane Finch."

"What? You mean York?"

"Yes! That's the one!"

"Did I tell you where SHE'S from?"

"I would love to chat all day with you honey, but your father is going to be home soon and the house is a mess, so I've got to get to work! Anyways you tell her not to eat all afternoon! I'm going to stuff both your faces! And tell her to wear that wonderful emerald necklace you got her! I want to see how it looks!"

"Okay mum I will. And Mum. I'm going to call Uncle Patrick – he's going to come for a visit to see you take your pills."

"What? Patrick's coming! My Patrick? All the way from Quebec?"

"Yeah Mum. Tell him I said hi. I love you. And happy birthday! I'll be home soon okay?"

"You too sugarplum. See you in a bit."

Facebook search: Lauren + York University= 2300 hits. I browsed the first twenty pages.

No Dice...

* * *

I got thinking about my brother Matt, and the day he was killed, eleven years ago next week.

As the eldest, he had always been the toughest, really it was no surprise. He'd been the first kid to take beatings, back while Nick and I were still wearing diapers.

He was also the only one to never begin drinking. He always said he didn't want his future kids to grow up in a house like we had. So even when he was out at neighborhood parties with gorgeous girls begging him to do shots off their breasts, he'd stick to a can of pop.

He found his outlet through physical altercation. He had his black belt and when he wasn't sparring on the provincial circuit, he was cruising the east side bars, looking for bullies twice his size to kick the shit out of. By eighteen he'd racked up ten assault charges, but none of them ever stuck. All the guys he'd put in hospital were burnt out wife-beaters the jury agreed weren't worth protecting.

He wanted to get his MBA and make a million on Bay Street. He'd enrolled in a business program at Ryerson and was getting straight A's. A couple of the major accounting firms were offering him internships.

I was sixteen and had just taken the worst beating of my life and it hadn't even been my father responsible. A broken nose, jaw, collarbone, four ribs and right arm plus a mild skull fracture. It took nearly a year to fully recover.

Everyday Matt begged me to tell him who had done it, promising he'd find them, make sure they could never hurt me again. Dad always said real men never snitch, but one day I caved in and told him everything that had happened. As soon as I did I felt infinitely better. I'd seen Matt smash a cinder block with his left hand. Other than my father, I was convinced he could take anyone. He had once taken a swing at dad in front of all of us – my father had caught Matt's hand in midair and shattered it like fine crystal with a single squeeze.

I know Matt went to dad's dresser and took the magnum he had stashed there. No one really knows what happened after that.

They never caught the killer.

My mother didn't sleep for six months.

I never told her it was because of me.

Looking back, I don't even remember why I was beat up. But I pray it was for something worthwhile.

CHAPTER TWENTY-FIVE

ADAM HAD BEEN back in Toronto for a few weeks but hadn't reached out, nor had he responded to my numerous text messages. I got the impression he was avoiding me.

He and I had been inseparable during those adolescent years, if anyone could provide some info, it was him. I got through on the fifteenth ring.

"Adam!"

"Sean?" He seemed surprised to hear from me.

"Hey man. It's been a while, how's it going?"

"Sean, I can't talk right now, me and Jan, we're" A giggle in the background, then a rustle of a bed sheet. "We're you know? Busy."

He could get laid later-I had important matters to address. "Adam. I think you're right, I think my memory is all out of whack."

He paused for a second-I could hear him saying something to Jan in the background "So you saw my guy, right?"

"No. Hell no. I don't wanna see some shrink."

"He's not a shrink, he's a Neurologist. They're completely different."

"Whatever, I don't need some high priced doctor. Things are coming back to me, I think."

"Sean, look I'm glad you're accepting it, but you gotta go see him, okay? With your mom, you of all people should know this. Professional help is the only way to go about it."

"No. Look. I think I'm on to something I just need help remembering it. Do you remember a girl named Lauren?"

He paused again and then spoke tenderly. "Sean."

"Just humor me. I think that's HER name, the girl I've been seeing around the city. You know? The brunette? Just tell me what the deal was. Was SHE my ex? Do you know HER last name? I think if I could just talk to HER, it would really help. I gotta find HER."

He took a deep breath, right into the receiver. "Sean. Go see him. I am not going to have this conversation. I can't have it again."

"Come on Adam, please."

I could hear her screaming in the background.

"Sean I have to go."

"Wait!"

There was a violent rustling of the phone. "Sean?" It was Jan, her tone riddled with frustration and resentment. She had always hated me. She was a diva who needed constant attention and I was the biggest detractor from his.

"Hey Jan! Long time no talk. How are you?" And I hated the bitch right back, but I did my best to be nice.

"Sean. Adam and I are trying to have a romantic

evening together. I don't need you calling him and stressing him out, do you understand?"

"What? Stressing him out? I'm just asking for a favor."

"And he's done one for you already. So you have no reason to call and ruin our night," she said.

"What? What is your problem? I just wanna talk to him for like two minutes. Then you guys can screw like rabbits for the rest of the night."

"My problem? I don't like you Sean. I think you're a loose cannon, a bad influence. Frankly I don't want Adam hanging around with you."

"What are you now, his mother? He's a big boy, he can make his own decision, don't you think?"

"His own decisions? And look how that's worked out with you in past. You think I'm gonna let you get him in trouble? You think I'm gonna let all your problems and fuck ups rub off on *my* Adam? I don't think so!" I'd had it. There would be no more playing nice with this twat. Her repressive regime had destroyed a most valuable friendship. And for what? Her insecurity was so glaring, so pathetic.

"What are you talking about? Are you on your rag or what? You don't know me, if anything it's you that's ruining Adam. You know he used to have big dreams before he met you? Yeah! He wanted to be a screenwriter out in California, talked about it day and night from the time he was twelve. You're the reason he didn't go to L.A. with me to see that come true. And I'm the one who's the bad influence? Please!" We were supposed to get a two bedroom out there together, a place I had found online in Westlake, which seemed like a great deal: cheap and central, back when I knew literally nothing about the city or life in general. At twenty-two I had asked him to come with me, even offered him a cut of my first book if he helped me sell it, but Jan had told him no, told him he was never going to make it and that he should get a safe, steady job so he could raise a family. She wanted two kids, two cars and a house in the burbs before thirty and as she so often liked to brag: Janet always got what Janet wanted.

I expected her to argue with my claim. She didn't. Instead she spoke slowly, hitting every syllable with intent to injure. "You're sick in the head Sean. Really fucking sick. You're just like your Dad. So listen asshole. My Adam is never going to see you again. Come near us and I'll call the police."

What gave her the right! "What! You don't ever talk about my dad. You hear me? You don't ever talk about him. You don't know the first thing about it. You spoiled little brat. You fucking bitch!" What did she know? A sheltered only child from a comfortable middle class suburb, her parents-both lawyers, still happily married after forty years.

She disconnected.

I redialed but his phone had been shut off.

A few hours later I got a text from him, saying he wasn't allowed to see me anymore.

Chapter Twenty-Six

I DREADED IT FROM the very second I hopped on the Scarborough RT. It was a last resort, plain and simple – an emotional bank robbery, in and out, as quick and painless as possible.

Nick was home, no surprise there. He was sipping on a bottle of dirty rye at 2:15 pm on a Tuesday, dressed only in his boxers, watching porn in his basement apartment, located at the end of a dead end street ripe with barred windows and spray paint. He bragged how he was "too tough" to live anywhere else. The reality was no one else would rent to him. He'd already been tossed out of ten buildings in the central city. The landlords here were crack dealers-they didn't give a shit what he got up to so long as he always paid rent and never brought the police.

"Well, well. The fuck you want, Hollywood?" He opened his door only an inch, peering out at me with total contempt.

"I need to talk to you, man."

He was bashed up, even more than usual, his left eye was sealed shut, his two front teeth were chipped and there were bruises all over his chest. "Well I'm busy! Some of us still gotta work for a living!" As far as I knew, he'd never had a real job.

"You okay? What happened to your face?" I asked.

"None of your business, princess."

"Alright. Well can I just have like ten minutes of your time?"

He contemplated for a second. "Fifty bucks."

"What?"

"You want ten minutes? It's fifty bucks. Make it worth my while."

"Fine," I reached into my wallet and passed a bill through the crack.

"Pleasure doing business with you, come on in, make yourself comfortable, princess, I'll start the clock." He opened the door fully and then he set a timer on his cell phone.

I walked past the cracked glass table, it was covered in pot roaches and crack rocks and took a seat on the torn Lazy Boy – held together by half a roll of duct tape. Beside it was a wobbly nightstand with a sawed off shotgun resting on top.

"A hundred grand a year and you still live like this? You give it all to mum or what?" I asked him.

He didn't even look at me, just his watch." None of your fucking business. Nine minutes."

"I talked to mum. She hasn't been taking her pills."

He smirked. "She's fine. That condo of hers up on the mountain is a palace and she's close to Uncle Pat. Nothing to worry about." His voice reeked of jealousy, he wanted a condo too.

"She should be taking them, she brought up Matt."

"Matt?"

"Yeah."

He picked up a crack pipe, tossed one of the rocks from the table into it and lit up, taking long inhales and exhaling perfect smoke rings. "He always was the favorite. Bet she didn't even mention me, right?"

"You think about it still?"

Another inhale followed by a barrage of cough. "Think about what?"

"Matt. The day he died."

"What's the point? It's not gonna bring him back. He was a great guy. God would take him, no question."

"Yeah, for sure." I felt like the brief recollection had brought us a bit closer. I liked that feeling. I even considered asking for a hit from the pipe. Not because I wanted to get high, I just wanted the chance to share in an activity with him.

"I'm thinking of going out there, to Montreal, make sure she's okay." Looking back I don't know why I even mentioned it, I didn't need his approval.

"Don't bother. She don't wanna see you. After what you put her through I don't blame her."

"Excuse me? What I put her through?" I remembered quite vividly the nights she had been up till dawn crying because Nick was back behind bars. He'd been arrested for selling dope five times: each time he'd been apprehended by the very same cop on the very same street corner.

"She's old now, way too fragile to put up with anymore of your shit." He put the pipe down and picked up the remote, resuming the pornography he'd been indulging in before I got there. I caught a quick glimpse of it and it made me really uncomfortable-the guy was drilling her from behind while forcing her head into a filthy toilet bowl. Nick stared at it intently, licking his lips, running his hands dangerously close to his groin.

"You mind turning that shit off?" I asked him.

"Yeah, I do." He took another look at his phone. "Six minutes. You know what? Make it three-I got shit to do today." He reached his hand down his boxers and began to rub himself.

I wanted to argue about our mother but didn't need to see him climax. I told myself I'd be out of there in ninety seconds or less.

"You remember a girl named Lauren?" I asked.

He looked at me and smirked. "No shit."

"SHE was my girlfriend, right?"

"What?"

"Lauren, SHE was my girlfriend, right?"

He paused the TV and pulled his hand away from his dick. "What are you getting at?"

"Nothing. Look man, I've just been having trouble remembering some things. Was hoping maybe you could help me jog my memory?" I said, in a gentle tone.

He hadn't always hated me. There were plenty of photos of us as toddlers – in every one of them he was hugging me. I remembered one night when I was eleven – my father had been chasing me around the house with a baseball bat. Nick hid me under his bed and told me to keep quiet. Then he told my father he would take the beating for me.

He started to laugh. "Me, help you? Fuck you!

Time's up." I checked my phone – even by his revised timeline I still had two minutes.

I reached into my pocket and retrieved my wallet. "How much more do you want?"

He stood up and pointed to the door. "I don't need your fucking money! Get the hell out!"

"I've got three hundred on me. And I can get more."

He went over to the nightstand and grabbed the shotgun. "I said, get the fuck out!"

I knew he didn't have it in him to kill his own brother, then again he was blitzed. All it would take was one slip of the trigger finger...

I hustled to the door.

"I don't care what mom says, I ever see you again I'll kill you, Sean! You destroyed this family! Not Dad! You!"

"What the hell is your problem?"

He let off a warning shot into the ceiling.

I got the hell out of there.

Chapter Twenty-Seven

THEY STILL COULDN'T get a hold of Nate's mother so I went and picked him up in a rent by-the-hour Toyota. I wanted to scream at him, smack him upside the head and scare some sense into him, but I managed to keep my mouth shut.

I drove him down to The Bluffs, to a spot reminiscent of the one in his novelette and we took a seat on the jagged cliff, legs dangling over the edge.

"I used to come here when I was your age." I told him. "Whenever things got too bad to handle, it always put things in perspective. No matter what happens-these cliffs are still here, no matter how bad we mess things up – the waves keep on crashing against them. Life goes on…"

"I wasn't trying to die." He said. "I just wanted to sleep."

And so did I. When you're a writer your mind is working at a furious pace every waking second of every day. If you can give it something creative to feast on, it becomes bearable. But when you can't, your own life becomes the narrative-plot twists and climaxes are better left for the page. If a book becomes too dark you can slam it shut, buy something else, it's not as simple when your life becomes too dark. "I just took a few too many" he added.

I reached into my pocket and pulled out a USB key. I tossed it into his lap.

"What is this?" he asked.

"Ten Feet Down." I replied. "I've been working on this thing for over three years. I can't finish it. But I think you can." He was raw but I'd seen instances of brilliance in him. With a little direction his potential was limitless.

"What?"

"Give me the ending, Nate and I'll give you fifty percent of everything on it. Do you have any idea how much these things make? You'll be a millionaire before you're eighteen."

"Are you serious?"

"Yeah, I am. I'll help you, but I need you to take the steering wheel. What do you say?"

"Wow! I'll do my best." He said reluctantly.

"Nah, Nate. That won't be enough. Are you up for this?" I replied, aggressively.

He gripped the key in his hand. "Yeah, Sean, I am."

Feast on that, kid.

I drove him home, to a stale cookie cutter house in the center of a stale cookie cutter subdivision from the 1970's. His house's only distinguishable characteristic was the basketball net on the edge of the single car driveway, the backboard was shattered and broken beer bottles lay all around its base.

After I dropped him, I rolled up a few houses and

parked along the curb, hoping to catch a glimpse of his mother, the one too busy to visit her son in the hospital, though, he passed through the door alone.

Suddenly my phone vibrated.

New text message, unknown number: *Sean. I need you. Why are you doing this to me? Don't forget about me. Please come back home…Lauren XoXo*

As I drove out of his subdivision I caught a glimpse of a street sign: Ropar Drive. Ropar? I'd never been to Malvern before and yet it sounded oh so familiar. There used to be a Ropar in India but I had never been nor wanted to go. Was there a Ropar Drive in Los Angeles? I knew I was thinking too much, the way I usually do, so I drove home listening to some sports cast and a heated discussion about the use of visors in the Freeway Hockey League. I had no idea what the hell that was but it helped me zone out. The less I used my brain, the happier I became.

Lauren had once told me I would have made a great radio DJ. I didn't remember HER last name or how we met, but just then, I remembered that.

Chapter Twenty-Eight

THE FOLLOWING WEEK Nate came to my apartment in an unusually good mood.

He wouldn't tell me why, but after six beers he opened up. He'd met someone, a girl named Lindsay at a horror movie marathon at the Bloor Theater. He was supposed to take her out the following night. I wanted him to stay focused on the book, but when he came in with three new chapters, all of them solid, I figured he'd earned the night out.

I took him to the Eaton's Centre and bought him some decent clothes. Rented a Mercedes and booked him a nice Italian restaurant on my coin. I wanted him to make a killer impression.

"If this stuff wins her over right out the gate, she isn't worth your time, but you'll still have some fun." I said. "If she appreciates it but is more interested in what you're all about, she's a keeper."

The date went well. He got his first kiss at a poetry slam battle in the basement of a dive bar in Parkdale. When he told me going there was her idea, I told him not to let her go.

PART V

December 2013

Toronto, Ontario

CHAPTER TWENTY-NINE

THE FIRST TWO weeks of December were the last good ones I ever had. I wish I had enjoyed them more than I did.

Working sixteen hours a day, Nate and I punched out what was left of the novel. He'd write a few new chapters each day while pretending to pay attention at school and then we'd edit it together at my apartment that night.

His writing was fresh, aggressive and best of all it flowed so well with my own. No one other than me, him and maybe Mark could tell where mine ended and his began. Because behind the narrative, the prose, the punctuation, he really got it, his heart beat in tune with its. He capitalized the indirect references to HER without being told to. He never had to ask why.

When we finished it, I booked us the bar on the fifty-first floor of the Manulife Center to celebrate. It had the highest outdoor patio in the city and an incredible view of both the Downtown and Uptown skylines. I ordered us a bottle of Cristal to celebrate. We polished it in ten minutes and I ordered another two.

"God, Nate. You have no idea how much your life is gonna change. I can't wait to get you set up in Los Angeles, you'll love it there." I assured him. I already had a place in mind, a sweet two bedroom in Santa Monica I knew he'd love.

"What about school?" He said.

"Forget school! You're rich!"

"What about Lindsay?"

"Bring her!"

He laughed. "You're crazy man, SHE can't go. SHE'S not even allowed to stay out past eleven."

"Well then you'll do it distance, or you'll find a new girl in L.A." I said. "With a bestseller it won't take long."

He pretended to laugh but deep down the idea petrified him. He had known his girl but a few weeks and already he was willing to put his best interests second.

You used to be like him.

CHAPTER THIRTY

"SEAN! LISTEN BUDDY! I read the manuscript you sent me and baby it's brilliant! Brilliant! We're back in business!" Hanson eagerly proclaimed over a conference call. I'd never seen him this excited.

"What did I tell you, Mark? Huh? What did I tell you? There was nothing to worry about!"

"Well damn, I'm sorry I doubted you, Sean. This one was more than worth the wait! I can see this pushing two million copies international. Especially in Europe-they love this kind of mindfuck shit." He said. "Two questions: one: when are you coming back to L.A.? Two: who is Nathan Rode?"

"Nate? He's this kid, sixteen, very talented. Gave me the ending this thing so badly needed. Me and him are gonna head back in a few weeks, once he finishes his semester up. I want him involved in the process, Mark, fully involved. He's the next big thing."

"Well I wouldn't argue that. I may just look at signing him on his own deal."

"That'd be great, I'm sure he'd be thrilled."

"Alright, so enjoy your last few weeks up in

Canada and be ready to go all out when you come back, we've got a lot of work to do."

"You bet. I'll see ya soon."

"Take care, Sean."

"You too."

CHAPTER THIRTY-ONE

ON AN IMPULSE, I went up to North York, to York U, the city's second largest university.

I'd never been there before.

I walked around the campus, taking in the sights, scents and sounds.

At first it felt expectantly foreign.

But then when I had to piss I knew the closest bathroom.

When I was hungry, I knew the best place to grub quick and cheap inside that mall of a student center.

When I wanted a round, I knew the location of the Underground bar and what they had on tap.

A student asked me where the Schulich building was and I gave him exact directions.

I saw a lot of cute girls, every fifth one I thought was Lauren from the distance, but when they came within ten feet I realized they looked nothing alike, half of them weren't even brunette. Maybe I needed glasses. Maybe I was just so desperate to see HER again, I was willing to compromise.

When I got tired, I went over to The Pond and

took a seat along the water. When I looked to my side I saw a shadow had joined me, a feminine shadow with long flowing hair that keep tussling even though there wasn't the slightest occasion of wind. It sat down and nestled in close, resting its head in my lap. Even though it was just a reflection of light, I felt it, on me, in me, so I put my hands right through it and held it close and it serenaded me, until, with an extended blink of my dry eyes, it was gone.

* * *

The city was starting to get cold. Too many Cali winters had thinned my blood. So I went for some hot whiskey at Cul De Sac, a Kensington bar.

It was a small venue – a central bar with five stools, surrounded by eight tables and three couches, maybe enough room for forty people at capacity, it was really cozy.

I saw a beautiful girl enter. She was a bleach blond, nineteen or twenty, five-nine and busty. She looked around for a second and then took a seat next to me at the bar. She ordered a cocktail and turned to face me. I was so lonely I prayed she would say something, anything.

"Hey" She said, cheerfully.

"Hi." I replied, a bit cold, trying not to look too eager.

"How's it going?"

"Not bad. You?"

"Look. I'm sorry to bother you, but are you? Sean O'Connor? The author Sean O'Connor?" Someone recognizing me here in Canada? My stomach clamped up.

"Yeah. That's me." I said nonchalantly while jumping up and down within my mind.

"You know? The book jacket doesn't really do you justice."

"Thanks." I tried to appear disinterested, it was the "cool" thing for celebrities to do, but it didn't work, I could feel myself blush and become a bit chubbed.

"You're really good, and I'm not just saying that. I had to read your stuff for contemporary English lit last semester. It was pretty solid. You must be proud." Chance of bedding her, 95 percent.

"You're too kind, Ms.?"

"I'm Cassie." She stuck out her hand.

"Pleasure." I shook it back, it was soft and silky, her wrist ripe with a perfume that made me want to eat her alive. I gave it a soft kiss and she giggled.

"So what brings you to this neck of the woods, Sean? I thought you lived in L.A.?"

"I do. I'm just back to finish a project."

"*Ten Feet Down*?"

I was pleasantly surprised-maybe she could start up a Toronto chapter of my fan club. "Bingo!"

"That's interesting. You know, it's got a lot of hype built up around it eh, think you can meet it?"

"I'm not too worried." Nate and I had turned out a solid product.

"That's good. So listen, this might be kinda forward but, I'm sorta on my way to this party, do you maybe wanna come? It's a whole bunch of English students-you'd be the guest of honor and it would make me look about ten times cooler."

. "Yeah sure, why not?" The only thing waiting for me at home was a mickey of rye.

"Cool. Let's go!"

That was too easy.

I'm famous – it's supposed to be easy.

Just decline and go home.

Piss off.

I was so freaking horny, both for sex and admiration. With a rack like hers (huge and exposed by a double push up), I would have followed her to hell and back. I never was one for the credo: never take candy from strangers.

She led me, her hand firmly on my pinky out of the bar and into her Honda Civic.

"Where are we going?" I asked.

"It's a surprise, silly!"

She drove us out of the central city, way out. I don't know where. We got talking about *Anything for a Dollar* and I stopped paying attention to anything but the praise. One minute we were driving west on the Gardiner, the next, we were on a quiet suburban street, each house indistinguishable from the next.

"People don't party in the city anymore?" I said, jokingly.

"With real estate prices these days? Who can afford to?" Touché.

There's no cars parked on the street?

We parked the car along the curb and she texted someone on her IPhone.

"So whose party is this?" I asked as we exited the vehicle.

"You always ask so many questions?"

"I'm a writer – it's my job to be inquisitive."

She pushed me up against the car and kissed me, firmly on the lips as she slid one hand down my chest to my groin.

She was aggressive, biting my lip, squeezing my cock with one hand while running the nails of her other over my back. It was pretty hot.

"You know? I've always wanted to fuck someone famous. You're not Michael Crow" I Googled him after, he scored the winning goal for Canada in the World Junior Hockey tournament last year. "But, you'll do just fine. When we get there, let's find a bedroom, okay?" She said, with a feverish pitch.

"Sure." And with that newfound full out erection, every doubt evaporated into thin air.

She led me, with a smile, a wink, and a flash of her red bra strap, up to one of the houses. The door was unlocked so we let ourselves in.

There's no shoes at the door?

Shut up. I need this.

She closed the door behind us, grabbed my index finger and with gentle force led me through the foyer and into the family room, where she pushed me onto a sofa.

"No one's here yet. Let's have a bit of fun before they get here." She giggled, straddling me.

She pulled off her top-her breasts looked even larger without it.

"You like?" She asked me.

"Oh ya!"

She removed her bra and then pulled my head

right into her chest "Kiss them, baby. Suck them for me." She pleaded.

I didn't want to be rude. So I did, indulging in every inch as she let off laughs and moans. They tasted like peaches.

I reached down for her pussy and she shoved my head back against the wall. It was then that I noticed there were three men standing calmly behind her, watching me.

"What the hell?"

"Sorry baby. There's been a change in plans." She replied with a dirty laugh.

"Cassie? What the hell is going on?"

She winked at me, got up and put her shirt back on. She didn't bother with the bra-she just forced it into a pocket.

"Cassie?"

"Sorry, gotta run, hun." She walked over to the three men and they handed her a wad of cash, she thanked them and ran out of the room.

They were big guys, all over six feet and at least 220 pounds. They were each dressed in a faded leather jacket and calmly smoking. "How's it going?" I asked them, trying to be casual.

"Shut up!" One of them ordered.

"Look guys, if you want my wallet, I don't have much cash on me. You can have a phone though?" I pulled it and the wallet out of my pants and placed them on the table in front of the couch. "Go for it, all yours."

"Just sit there and keep your mouth shut, he'll be here soon."

"Who?"

The guy had a killer jab – it rocked my head back against the wall. My vision went blurry, a buzzing noise filled my ears.

"No more fucking questions!"

I thought about running, but curiosity got the better of me. Deep down, an audience begged to see this play out in as dramatic a fashion as possible.

After five minutes, I could hear the front door open and the footsteps soon gave way to a smaller, slimmer "mystery man". I say mystery because I had no clue who the hell the guy was. Frankly I was expecting it to be Nick, wielding a shotgun, calling me "a princess" before taking my head clean off. But no, this guy certainly wasn't my coke fiend brother. His appearance in general was nothing unusual. He was of average height, average build, had average hair, dressed in average clothes. He was just an average middle class Torontonian. He didn't look dangerous save for a look in his eye, a look that said this wasn't random, this was personal. He took position in front of the three goons and smiled.

"Hey Sean, it's been a long time." He spoke in an average voice.

"Sorry? Do I know you?"

He started to laugh, hysterically. "That's funny. In addition to that shitty writing, you do standup now too?"

"Buddy, I hate to blow your grand reveal, it looks like you put a lot of thought into this little charade, but I got no clue who you are." I responded casually.

He smirked "Thought? Nah. Everyone and their mother knows what it takes to get you off your guard."

"Aw, and here I am thinking she liked me for me." I said, sarcastically.

"Who could ever like a prick like you? Anyways enough of this bullshit – cut the act. You're trying my patience, Sean."

"Sure, once you tell me who the hell you are."

He starred into my eyes without saying a word.

"Huh. You're not lying. Maybe you drank away the brain cells huh? That sounds about right. Not that you ever had many to begin with." The four of them laughed. "He reached into his jacket pocket and pulled out a 9mm which he promptly cocked and pointed at my head. "What do you think it will take, to help you remember? Huh? You think a bullet could do it?" First and only instinct, do not get shot again.

"Woah! Woah! Relax buddy! Whatever this is about, we can work it out. What is it? I owe you some money? That's it right? How much? We can go down to the bank right now and work it out." Money and sex, the only two reasons a man is ever killed and he wasn't my type.

The offer only enraged him further. "Money? No. You wish it was about money. No, you can't just buy your way out of this."

"Then what the hell do you want?"

He stepped forward and smashed me across the face with the pistol. I could hear my jaw crack on impact.

He screamed passionately. "I want her back! I want everything you took from my family back!"

He pulled my head up by the chin and placed the gun against my forehead. To both his and my dismay, the altercation was doing nothing to spur my memory—to me he was still just the average Torontonian.

"Now how do you reckon you can do that, smart guy" He mocked. "You a magician too?" He pushed the barrel harshly into my skull. "I've been waiting for this a long time, now say goodnight." I closed my eyes, wondering what I would see this time.

There was a police siren in the background – loud and clear.

"Dave. Cool it a second." One of the muscle commented.

"What?" Dave turned to inquire.

As soon as he was off guard, I pushed the gun away from my face and I hit him, square on his cock and threw the prick backwards, right onto a glass table which shattered on his dramatic impact.

Before the muscle could respond, I booked it for the door, not looking back, expecting to take one or two bullets in the process. But I caught a break – I didn't even hear a shot. When I got outside I tore up the pavement. I kept looking over my shoulder but there was nothing but trees and SUVs behind me. When I got to the nearest intersection, I stopped to catch my breath.

I wanted to get another look at him. I waited there for ten minutes but neither he nor his muscle ever showed up.

* * *

I was on a major street in some suburb, who the hell knew which one? I passed a Canadian Tire, a

McDonalds, a Sobeys, a Starbucks and a Tim Hortons, they were all closed. I was the only one out on the sidewalk.

Cars whizzed by at twice the speed limit. I stuck out my thumb. No one stopped. One Escalade full of frat boys called me a faggot and whipped a bottle of vodka at my head, I ducked just in time and it smashed against a telephone pole.

Eventually, I caught sight of the lake-I figured I'd just follow it, hoping sooner or later, it would bring me back to civilization.

The sidewalks out here were so clean, so polished, here just for decoration.

But something stood out. Didn't belong. A few feet in front of me was a single tile, painted black and in its center was a light red star. It read "Sean O'Connor." Underneath it was a metal emblem of a book.

It was a Hollywood Star.

There had been a time when this had been my dream.

PART VI

2006-2007

Los Angeles, California

Chapter Thirty-Two

Los Angeles.

A S A KID, it was all I ever talked about. Growing up on the other side of the continent, in another country at that, my vision of La La Land was, as it is with most, founded solely on the mass media's sensational, value added branding. For me, someone who had never been there, it was the greatest place on earth.

On frigid days in February, I warmed up by picturing myself on Santa Monica Beach, body submersed in the soothing sand, kept comfortable by droplets of refreshing water blown off the ocean.

When I felt lonely, I imagined myself surrounded by an adoring entourage on Hollywood Boulevard. Beautiful people who loved me for the talent I was yet to make viable.

When I was horny, I pictured the gorgeous cougars from Beverly Hills-looking for an exotic young writer to make their pet, their sex slave, while their

Viagra-addicted husbands slaved through hundred hour work weeks to meet the mortgage.

When I was sad, I thought of L.A. and how things would finally be okay once I got myself under its all-powerful, protective sphere.

And then, as a dumbfounded twenty-two year old, I finally went there.

I got into LAX at a quarter to nine at night. The sky had already adopted a foreboding shade of black, so dark that the palate of the sky remained utterly blank. You never see the stars in this town.

I strutted up to the terminal's tourist information desk, a stupid smile on my face "Excuse me. Where can I get a bus to Hollywood?" I asked.

He looked up at me, then down at me. "First time in L.A.?"

"Yeah! Just got in from Canada."

A deep exhale. "You'll want to go grab yourself a cab, there's plenty outside."

It was the middle of December and yet, the air was a soothing twenty degrees, my excitement barely contained under the roofs of countless, picturesque palm trees, that would never have to die under the thrashing of a harsh northern climate.

"You on duty?" I asked the cab at the front of the cue. I had never taken a cab before. I considered it a luxury item.

"Sure am. Hop in kid."

He took my bags without me bothering to ask and placed them gently into the trunk.

We started driving, hopping onto the freeway, heading eastbound towards the Downtown skyline-it looked gorgeous against the dark canvas of the sky. "First time in L.A.?" he asked.

"Yeah. I just moved out here. From Toronto."

"Where?" It was a common reaction.

"Canada."

"Ah okay. Here for the sunshine and beautiful blonds I take it?"

We shared a laugh.

"Something like that."

"So where am I taking you? Santa Monica? Beverly Hills? The South Bay? The Valley? Cause I don't serve north of The Hills"

"What's The Valley?"

"The San Fernando Valley. But locals don't call it that."

"Oh, right." I nodded and pretended to know what that meant.

"Don't worry about it-you'll pick up the lingo. So where to? I see you as a Westwood kinda guy actually. Am I right? You here for UCLA?"

"Hollywood."

"West Hollywood?"

"I dunno. My apartment is near Hollywood and Gower? Is that West Hollywood?"

"Hollywood and Gower?" His tenor shifted. He sounded startled.

I looked down at the lease agreement, the one I'd negotiated online. "Yeah. That's what my note says. "

"Why do you wanna have an apartment there?" A judgmental tone.

"Why not?" The rent was reasonable, there was a

subway stop close by and plenty of nightlife to indulge in. It was perfect.

"You couldn't pay me to live in *Hollyweird*. But each their own I guess." He said.

We got to my building. A no frills three story walk up on a residential street between Hollywood and Sunset. He grabbed my bags and I tipped him 20 percent.

"Hey kid, take some advice, don't go walking around this area at night, okay?" He said.

"Why not?"

He got back in the car. "Just trust me."

I was still a child, still naïve and hopelessly idealistic, anxious to finally find my place in the world. But all I found in Hollywood were several thousand other, young, naïve and idealistic individuals, all desperate for a societal womb to find warmth, and a few hundred, old, bitter, remorseless sharks, eager to tear us to shreds while we struggled to tread water amidst the roaring tide.

The glitz and glamour were long gone, all that was left was a tourist trap riddled with the city's scraps. I expected to see film premieres every night of the week – but, it turned out, the only nightly presentation was that of the homeless, proudly urinating on the cracked cement stars, representing cultural idols who wouldn't be caught dead there without the presence of extensive security and/or hundreds of cameras.

The media uses the titles of Los Angeles and Hollywood interchangeably, but I do want to stress, they are NOT the same thing. Hollywood is but a neighborhood, one piece of the much larger mosaic that is the city of Los Angeles, which is itself only one piece of the much larger Los Angeles County. Important people live in Los Angeles County. Important people live in the city of Los Angeles itself. Important people do not live in Central Hollywood.

It had gotten a lot better since the eighties and nineties. They'd just built a megamall at the corner of Hollywood and Highland and I saw a few signs for million dollar condos in pre-construction near the intersection of Hollywood and Vine, gentrification was en route. Still, I carried this incredible tension in each and every muscle as I walked its streets. This sense of dread, as if some dark presence was lurking under the star covered concrete. Wherever I was going, I couldn't get there fast enough. I got great at speed walking-I figured maybe I'd try out for the Olympic team.

The heart of the neighborhood is The Boulevard: a dense street, packed with tacky tourist shops, historic movie theaters, overpriced restaurants and trendy bars. When you're without a car it's where you spend most of your time. During the day it's okay. The repulsive stench of con artists, bums and addicts is still strong, but with the dumbfounded tourists, who flood the Boulevard between La Brea and Vine, there's enough tacky perfume in the air to make it manageable. You won't get nauseous, so long as you just keep your eyes to the gorgeous horizon. But when night falls, it's a whole new game. My first night there a tourist was stabbed to death by a crackhead's sharpened tooth brush. The killer told police he thought she was possessed by the devil.

Things get better, a lot better once you cross La Brea

into West Hollywood, a completely separate city with a lot more charm and a lot less grime. I went there a lot, and I'd pretend it was my neighborhood. I'd write in its cafés, drink in its bars, flirt with its women, really begin to enjoy myself. But then the bars would close and reality would set in. I didn't belong here, I was a broke nobody, I had to head back east.

My tenth night I was coming back from the Sunset Strip and crossed over La Brea at around 1 am. The tourists had gone back to their hotels long ago and the locals were, as always, driving from doorstep to doorstep. All that was left were the homeless and the whackos. There was a skinny old man dressed only in his boxers-he was cutting his arm open with a piece of broken glass, claiming aliens had implanted a chip there. Then there was a young guy, dressed in a Santa outfit screaming on about how the world would end tomorrow if he didn't sodomize a Terrier. There were also a couple of six foot trannies ripe with cold sores, who flashed me their dicks, claiming once I'd be penetrated I'd never go back. There was a reason they called the area "Hollyweird".

It freaked me out but it also amused me. I figured it would all be great material for a book. I walked fast and kept my eyes to the starless sky. If you looked like nothing phased you, they left you alone.

Usually.

A guy marched up to me and grabbed me by the shoulder. He had on a leather jacket-open a smidge to reveal his bare well defined abs above torn jeans, a cigarette dangling carelessly from one side of his mouth, while he occupied the other with a bottle of bourbon.

He pulled his jacket open further and revealed to me two handguns and a machete on his waist. "You see this? This is real shit. You know what this is right?" He said.

I tightened up. I hadn't been mugged since leaving Scarborough, I was out of practice. "No."

He grinned "I see you around, I know ya new in town so I'm gonna do you a solid and escort ya home."

"I'm good man. Thanks." I tried to walk on but he pulled me back.

"Nah man, you ain't. You see that?" He pointed towards a Cash Outlet across the street. Nothing spectacular, the area was full of places to pawn your stuff or borrow cash at exuberant interest rates.

"Yeah."

"You see 'em?"

"Who?"

"Look closer, man."

I looked at it again, longer this time, and sure enough there was a guy sitting in front of the store, resting on top a container providing free Movie Star Maps. He was a big guy, over 300 pounds, wearing a Lakers Jersey and a bandana, eyeing me while taking long puffs from a joint. His giant nostrils flared. He was smelling me, the fear right off me, when I caught his eyes he blew me a kiss.

"You mean that guy?"

"Yeah man."

"Who is he?"

"Look man like I said, I'm doing y'all a favor, this one time. You shouldn't walk through Hollywood alone at night, not unless ya suicidal, aite?"

"Ok..."

He walked me back to my apartment in silence, keeping one hand on a gun the entire time while he ran the machete against the sidewalk concrete. He waited for me on my doorstep until I got inside. I didn't say thank you, even though I should have, I was way too shook up. The guy over by the Cash Outlet could have mugged me, stabbed me, raped me. Maybe all of the above?

After that, I was home behind my bolted door every night by nine. I didn't have a TV there, or internet, but I did have a fridge.

I like the liquor stores in Los Angeles. Especially the ones in Hollywood, unlike everything else in this town, they're honest. They don't try to mask their true nature with glitz, glamour or marketing. They're grungy, depressing and often times violent. The cashier is kept behind an inch of bulletproof glass. You know why you're there.

And, more importantly, they're cheap. Bye bye Canadian taxes. Hello bliss on a writer's wage. I like the portions too. The place I frequented, the smallest quantity available was a liter tall can, and those generally only came in two packs.

It was all domestic, save for the occasional Mexican brew, it was all junk and yet for some reason, even at a lower percentage, it got me a lot more messed up than the premium stuff you could find at the LCBO back in Toronto. I'd grab three of these duo packs every afternoon, the tally less than $10 and would spend the nights alone getting buzzed as I watched out my window at the action on the street. A lot of people parked their cars on it so there was always free entertainment: cracked out guys singing, bar stars brawling, horribly failed pickup attempts. Every few nights I'd see a car get broken into as part of a smash and grab. Once in a while it would be straight up stolen. Occasionally you'd see a mugging.

The only real constant was this one working girl who passed my building every night on her way to and from Santa Monica Blvd. She had six inch heels and torn lace fish nets, along with a faded blue dress. She was twenty-five but looked forty, still, she was actually very pretty. I never spoke to her, but seeing her each night, even for an instant, made me feel a little less alone.

CHAPTER THIRTY-THREE

I FOUND WORK AS a dishwasher at a rundown diner on Sunset-a relic of the golden age now catering to tourists and the underclass. They had a statue of Marilyn Monroe and every item on the microwaved menu was named after someone with a star on the Boulevard. The bottom of the tables was full of used gum and the kitchen ran rabid with roaches. Still, it paid cash and accepted Northern Aliens.

I met a waiter there named Dan. He was a few years older and a lot more jaded. He was from Toronto too so he offered to show me around. He was going to a party in The Hills and told me I should tag along to start building some bridges.

"There a bus going up there?" I asked.

"A bus?" He laughed. "Fuck no, where's your wheels?"

They all had cars. I'm pretty sure I was the first sane person since 1950 to live in the city without one. Most of the other starving artists had gotten one as a gift from their parents before they left. The rest picked up junkers with 300,000 km on them once they arrived. There's a saying in L.A: "Better to have a Benz and live on the street, then to have a mansion and ride your bike." But, I was a stubborn asshole and a city boy, I didn't need a car. I shouldn't need one, no one here really should, I mean come on – this was the third biggest city on the continent (including Mexico)!

"Alright, I'll pick you up around 11. Where do you live?"

I gave him my address.

He texted me at 11:10, saying he couldn't find my street. He asked if I could walk up to Hollywood, I said I'd meet him at Gower.

I was dressed in my best outfit: a dress shirt missing its top two buttons and a pair of tight black jeans with a tear near the ankle. I waited anxiously alone on the sidewalk, counting every second, knowing damn well I shouldn't be here, not now. I could feel the discomfort nagging in my bones. It was funny, because the area didn't look bad at all. The buildings were pretty well maintained, I couldn't see any public housing, there wasn't too much gang graffiti and the Walk of Fame was right under my feet. The ghettos on the east coast look decayed, in L.A. it's not the look that gives it away, it's the ambiance, I breathed it in and my lungs quivered in consternation.

The neighborhood was silent save for the roaring indifferent traffic, at first all the cars provided me comfort and companionship, before I realized that no one looks out their windows in L.A.

I felt a tap on my shoulder. I figured it was Dan.

It wasn't.

"Hey man, you got some rock, buy or sell? What about some smack? Blow? Weed? What you got?" He was tall and skinny, dressed in a black hoodie which concealed his face.

"No. Sorry man."

"What you say?"

"I don't have any drugs, I don't want any either."

He shoved me back a few feet and started to bark. "Why you lying to me, motherfucker? Pretty little bitch like you out alone in Hollywood at night don't want nothing but rock or hoes and the girls are down on Santa Monica!"

"Look man, I'm just waiting for a friend alright, I don't want any trouble."

"Yeah, well, trouble just found you tourist faggot. Unless maybe you loan me $50. Cause I could use a new pair of shoes, know what I mean?" I looked down at his feet, he already had a pair of brand new Nikes, all I had was a $30 pair of loafers, if anything, I should be mugging him.

I kept calm and just starred him down, in an attempt to show him I wasn't afraid. I was taller and broader – if it came to it I figured I could kick his ass. He was probably used to dealing with the babbling yokels. The ones who thought The Eiffel Tower on the Las Vegas Strip was the real thing. For them, he would have been petrifying. I compared all men to my father and my dad could have killed this scrawny fiend with a single punch.

He could tell I wasn't going to concede and so he snapped his fingers and three more guys with nearly his identical description popped out of seemingly nowhere, they surrounded me on all sides and began circling me like a pack of wolves. I looked off down the street, but there were no other pedestrians, no witnesses anywhere.

"Your wallet, passport, phone, everything, put it on the concrete right now, motherfucker." One of them ordered, as casual and indifferent as an airport security officer telling you to remove your belt and shoes for the metal detector.

And then Scarborough logic kicked in.

"No." I said firmly, standing upright, cocking my head.

"What you say to me?"

"I said no. I'm not giving you anything."

"Fucker, you wanna die? You crazy? Shit, where you from?"

"I come from a place where it's like this: no knife? No gun? Go fuck yourself!" It worked in Toronto, more often than not. If they had something they would have already shown it, I figured.

Then, all four pulled out handguns.

"That enough gun for you, motherfucker?" One asked rhetorically.

"Yeah. That's enough."

While I emptied my pockets, I watched the traffic at the stop-light and the cold, unsympathetic faces of a wealthy WASP family in a Jaguar on their way back to the west side. I made eye contact with the mother in the passenger seat, but she didn't have an ounce of sympathy for me, her pupils completely disinterested. It wasn't that she was hollow-it was that to her

I didn't exist. On the other side of the glass, nothing did. Every other passenger in every other car felt the same way. In L.A., society doesn't extend beyond your automobile, the world outside nothing more than a channel, a channel you'll change as soon as the light turns green.

They grabbed everything as quickly as they could, tossing it into a nearly full laundry bag, they'd had a profitable evening indeed.

"On your knees! Kiss the fucking pavement." He waved the gun at me.

Before I could retort, one struck me on the back of the head with a handle.

And then on the star studded pavement, they stomped me furiously while the traffic just kept flowing, undisturbed. Their only concern was that the violence stay on the sidewalk, God forbid it move to the street and they find their two hour commute increased a few minutes.

When they were done, they ran to a nearby parked car and drove off. I got back on my feet, slowly, gripping my rib cage, as pain radiated out of my lungs with each blood soaked cough. I let out a spit of plasma onto a star of some comedian from the 50's.

Why haven't all these stars been stolen yet?

A car drove up beside me. It was Dan. Riding shotgun was another guy from the restaurant, in the backseat were two cute girls. Dan rolled down the window and started laughing. "Jesus Christ, you look like fucking roadkill!"

I tried to speak, the pain in my chest was insurmountable, all I could do was groan.

"What the hell is his problem?" One of the girls asked.

"Whatever it is, I'm not being seen with him," said the other. "Dan! Let's go! I don't wanna be late!"

Dan rolled up the window and drove away.

CHAPTER THIRTY-FOUR

AFTER THE MUGGING, I didn't leave my stuffy little studio apartment after 8 pm for anything, upping the intake from six cans to ten. The hooker in the blue dress stopped coming by. Apparently they found her headless a few feet from the Hollywood sign.

I was a city boy, but this wasn't a city, it was a collection of suburbs. Funny thing is, this town used to be one of the densest around, a walkable city with great public transit. Until the 1950's and the push north to the San Fernando Valley and the glossy new dream of suburbia: in search of the big house, the big backyard, the big Chevy, the hourglass housewife, the American Dream. Now, most of The Valley was comprised of no go areas. Some of them were considered a lot rougher than Hollywood.

I grabbed buses with ninety-cent fares out to the ocean and that made me happy. I thought about moving to Venice, but didn't. After dark the beach there were just as bad as Hollywood Blvd, hell, even Santa Monica beach was supposed to be terrible at night. I didn't understand how the millionaires who owned mansions out by the Pacific Coast Highway could sleep at night, in their ten million dollar plus estates, knowing an open drug market operated a stones throw from them. But that was just it, for a city with the best weather in the world – no one gave a damn about the state of the outdoors. If it didn't have air conditioning it wasn't worth protecting. I didn't get it.

But I did send copies of each one of my works to every major publisher in the country. I expected a bidding war, but the only thing I got back from any of them was an envelope marked "return to sender".

So I went to the agents. I mean that was why I came to this city in the first place, the contacts. I called about fifty of these guys and got five calls back, I went to see them later that week.

"This is amazing work! Honestly, I couldn't put it down!" He had a gigantic smile and a tremendous energy-it was enough to compensate for his misplaced toupee and a wrinkled suit that reeked of bourbon. His tiny office was a complete mess, papers and file folders were sprawled out everywhere without any rhyme or reason, outnumbered only by the half-empty packages of cigarettes of at least ten different brands.

"Really? Thanks, that means a lot!" I said back eagerly from the other side of his desk.

"Yeah, I mean kid you got it, the gift, you got it in bundles."

"Thank you! Which one did you like the best?"

He gave a nervous laugh. "Which what?"

"Book?"

He slammed his hand down on his lap

enthusiastically. "Oh! Yeah! Well I kinda loved them all."

It was a complete red flag, but at the time I was far too caught up in his praise to be rational.

He reached into his desk and retrieved a form which he placed out in front of me. "So, I wanna sign you ASAP." He grabbed a pen as well and placed it on the form.

"Really?" I lit up and could barely keep myself in his cold iron chair.

"Oh yeah, for sure. Let's get these puppies on the shelves! Make us some real money!"

"Yeah, let's do this!" he stuck out his calloused hand and I shook it repeatedly, his palm was greasy, his grip lazy.

"Great! Before we get rolling, there's a few things we have to sort out, nothing major, just a little paper work. You know what they say, all good things require signatures."

I looked down at the paper for the first time, it had tiny font and lots of it, the text I could make out made no sense what so ever, legal jargon I figured only a practicing lawyer could comprehend. "Is this my contract?" I asked him, squinting my eyes to try and make out some more of it.

"Yeah, exactly. Well I mean sorta. It's kinda like that. It's for your signing fee, just sign off at the bottom, attach a check and we're golden."

"What? A signing fee? Aren't you supposed to give me that?'

He started to lark, until he lit a cigarette to calm himself down, blowing the smoke across the table and into my face. "What? Who told you that? Anyways it's nothing too big, $750."

"What? I don't have that kinda money."

He pulled the paper back, just slightly out of my reach. "No? Well that's a shame. I smelt a best seller. Maybe you can take out the money? There's plenty of loan places in Hollywood."

'But isn't the interest on that stuff crazy?"

He kept the smile and the energy, but it didn't feel empowering any longer, he was a used car salesman, nothing more. Worse, he didn't care if I plain walked off the lot empty handed. Everyone in this town needed a ride. "Hey, that's just how she goes. I can't get going without something up front, my time's too valuable. If you're not willing to invest in me, in yourself, then go see someone else." He picked up his cell phone and began to text someone, he didn't bother to look at me again as I walked out.

The only ones willing to see me, all gave me the same shtick. They were located in different buildings on different streets in different neighborhoods but they were like a franchise, the treatment you received was consistent. I figured they likely all trained at the same seminars. At first I figured forget them, I knew I was good, I could make it alone. But after another fifty or so nights spent alone in that tiny anxious waiting room of an apartment, with nothing to do but get drunk and hope for entertainment outside my window, I got desperate enough to give in.

I had $500 left in seed money and I came up with the rest by selling my watch, my silver chain, my suitcase and even some of my nicer pieces of clothing.

I had two weeks to come up with $800 for rent – otherwise I'd be out on the street. There was an abandoned couch sitting in an alleyway just off Hollywood Blvd. It was torn in multiple places and stained in piss and liquor, but would provide some back support. It beat the sand. There had been a bunch of videos on YouTube of rich kids beating the homeless on Venice Beach half to death for fun. I really didn't want to make a cameo.

I walked back into his zoo of an office and slammed the cash down on the table. "I got the money. The 750."

He cracked a huge smile and motioned for me to sit down, I did. He grabbed the cash and slipped it into his pocket, then he brought the form out again and I signed it without bothering to try and read it. "Alright kid! Good for you! You won't regret it! So listen, next we need to work on your headshot."

"Why? I'm not an actor. Why would I need a headshot?"

He shrugged his shoulders "Doesn't matter, it's all about image in this town, kid, we need to create one for you. I mean no offense, but you walk into a studio, dressed like that and security is gonna toss you out on your ass, we need to give you some style." It seemed grossly inappropriate coming from him, he didn't even have a suit on, just a dress shirt that was two sizes too small, the cuffs sitting halfway between his elbow and his wrist.

The red alerts just kept coming and as desperate as I was, I couldn't keep looking past them. "Why would I go to a studio? Wouldn't I go to a publisher?"

"Studio! Publisher! Whatever tomato, tomato!

Anyways the headshot is from a friend of mine, he'll give us a discount, $400. Real good deal." He reached into his desk and retrieved another form-it looked identical to the last.

"400? I can't come up with that now. Why do we even need one, can't we just let the work speak for itself?"

He lit another cigarette and let it rest in his mouth while he placed his hands behind his head. "Come on kid. This is how it's done, okay?" The ashes started to fall onto his desk, he didn't seem to care. "With me, it's my way or the highway. You don't like it? Well there's the door." He pointed directly to it.

"I'll take the headshot myself. Okay? I'll get a camera and I'll take care of it. I'm a pretty good photographer. All right? Let's meet halfway."

He lost the corny smile and smashed his hands down on his desk so hard I could see his left began to bleed. Then he stood up and started screaming. "For Christ's sake, get out. Get the hell out! Fucking rookie! I can't work with you!"

"What?"

"Get out! I don't want you or your shitty writing!"

"You said you liked it."

"I didn't even read it! You think I have time for that? To read some loser's scribbles. Get real!" He picked up my manuscript and tore pages out of it before tossing it into his garbage can, where it lay among bloody tissues, cigarette butts and a condom wrapper.

I reached out my hand. "Okay so give me my down payment back."

"Excuse me?"

"The signing fee, the 750. Give it back and I'll go."

"You little shit, you trying to rob me?" He picked up his phone and quickly called the police. When I gestured for the phone, he gestured for his waistline, where he had a pistol waiting. I started to back up, one step after another until I was in the doorway.

"Yes, please help me! There's a guy in here, he broke in! He's crazy! I think he's got a gun. Oh my God!" He screamed into the phone before slamming it down onto the receiver. "Well, the cops are on their way."

I made my way back out to the street. As always, there was no one else on the sidewalk and the cars were driving pretty fast – no one looking out their windows. I grabbed a rock off the road's shoulder and hurled it at his window. The whole thing shattered, glass flying in every direction. I could hear him scream and curse. I hoped a piece had cut him.

CHAPTER THIRTY-FIVE

BETWEEN AN INFINITE array of rejection, I always made time, during the late afternoon, to sip Polish vodka from a plastic flask on the foothills of Griffith Park. It was a beautiful spot, a serene spot, the perfect place to get some fresh air. And it was there that I met him, my savior, Mark Hanson.

Back then, he was living in Los Feliz, where he routinely walked his golden retriever down Vermont Ave, every evening after work to blow off steam and cruise for available women.

Though that day, things didn't go exactly to plan. Two teenagers caught him alone.

"Hey man, you got a light?" The larger of the two asked him.

"For you?" Mark snapped back.

"Yeah for me, no shit, genius"

"Look, I'm busy, there's a liquor store five minutes from here, buy one yourself." He retorted, fearless as usual. He continued on his walk only to have the other one step out in front of him.

"You disrespecting me?"

He gave the kid a push. "Prick. I'm walking my dog, what's your problem?"

By the time I entered the frame, Mark had one pinned to the ground. He was hitting the punk so hard, the concrete was staining red. The other came up behind him, ready to issue a blow to the back of his head. I saw it all happening in slow motion. I had plenty of time to react.

"Hey!" I grabbed a bottle from a nearby trash-can and smashed it against the nearest lamp post-the sound got their attention, bringing it to the pretty imposing shank I'd created. They took a look at it, then at me. I was drunk-reckless. They misread this as confidence and they both started to run.

Hanson got back up to his feet and whipped his bloody nose onto the sleeve of his white dress shirt before looking at me. "Fuckers are gonna cost me another dry cleaning bill. Thanks kid. I owe you one."

"No problem."

"You know? This park used to be safe? Whole city is going to hell, about time I move myself up to The Hills."

I dropped the bottle and walked over to him. "You okay, man?"

"Me? Yeah, of course, I ain't made of glass. But hey, I've got a dog-he ran off during the fight. Help me look for him?"

"Sure." I've always liked helping people, plus, I was in no rush. I had five tall cans in the fridge, the longer they stayed there, the colder they got.

The pooch turned up, about twenty minutes into our search through the park, it was perfect timing. It gave us just enough time to shoot the shit and subsequently set something up.

"So what do you do, kid?" He asked.

"I'm a writer." I replied, expecting one of the usual sarcastic responses.

He smiled and gave me his full attention. "Really? Of what? Film? TV?"

"Novels."

"Oh ya? You any good?"

"I think so."

"So you published?"

"Not yet."

"Have an agent?"

"Ah man. I've been looking. But they all want so much money upfront. Like $500 to $1200. It's crazy. I'm broke."

He laughed and rolled his eyes. "What? You've been talking to some scam artists then. No real agent would take a fee, just a percentage."

"What, really?"

"Of course."

"Well I guess I haven't been able to talk to anyone credible yet. No one's taking my calls."

"You and thousands of others kid. You have a manuscript?"

"At home, yeah."

"Tell you what. I figure I owe you a couple. I'll give you my address, you should send it over. I've been looking to break into literary for a while now, diversify my portfolio. I'd be interested to see what you've got."

"Well I've got three books."

"Great, send them all. If I'm interested, I'll make you an offer, no signing fee involved. Just 15 percent."

"That seems fair."

And from there, things moved fast. Within three months we had three publishers biting. Within nine, I had my first novel on the shelf, a New York Times bestseller. Within a year, I was rich.

Los Angeles is two faced. When you're poor, it's a mountain and you're tumbling down, always gaining momentum, unable to latch on to anything as your bones begin to break one by one. But behind the gritty façade lays a wonderland invisible to the unsuccessful eye.

A world of prestige and exclusion, bland unmarked buildings housing the most lavish and extravagant inner finishing's. But, once inside, I was no longer young, things were no longer simple and everything wasn't okay.

Success is the inverse of those buildings. Outside: beautiful, glamorous, heavenly, the embodiment of every virtue ever taught. But inside: insipid, hollow, rotten.

PART VII

December 2011

Toronto, Ontario

Chapter Thirty-Six

I LOVE THE LIQUOR store at Summerhill.
Going there makes me feel like a kid in a toy store.

You walk in and face the vast beer selection: hundreds of varieties, in bottles and cans, in singles and packs, ripe with cool designs and hailing from dozens of countries around the world. I never know what to pick, usually I'll grab two varieties and duel them out like they were action figures. It really helps me blow off steam.

Walk further in and you'll see the spirits: the rum, the vodka, the tequila, the whiskey, the gin, the sake, the brandy and all the sexy derivatives they've spawned. Prices start in the teens, for mickeys of watery bar rails and go up to $26 000 for fifty year old Glenfiddich. The homeless bum and the CEO both find what they're looking for.

Then there's the wine. Thousands of bottles: corks and screw tops, new and vintage, red, white and rose. And there's the wine tasting station. As I wait for my turn I remember the electric toy train sets – carriage

going in the same loop for all eternity and how enam-
ored I was with it as a child.

You could spend hours in here, I usually do. The
owners don't mind. They offer wine appreciation and
cooking classes several nights a week.

Behind the billions spent on branding by market-
ers, behind the strategic shelving selections made by
account managers and the cute little ribbons tied onto
handles for show by morally neutral machines, we
all know what this shit is, what this shit does. But we
don't care. And when we lie to ourselves, we lie big,
we go all out, the sheer selection here can attest to that.
This whole place is like a casino, designed on a macro
and micro level to discard you of your better judgment
and play to your darkest desires. If you weren't thirsty
when you came in, you'll be parched by the time you
reach the register. Experts have seen to that.

* * *

I was so thrilled with my acquisitions that as I departed
Shangri-La I didn't even realize I was walking in the
wrong direction, until I hit St Clair.

My arms were getting tired.

So I migrated underground and took position on
the busy southbound platform.

The next train was said to arrive in three minutes.
It was rush hour. There was no way we'd all be able to
get on.

The lights began to aggressively flicker, creating a
strobe-like effect.

Then they went out altogether.

And came back on.

I looked across the tracks at the northbound platform.

SHE was there, standing at the front of the massive nine to five crowd.

"Lauren!" I yelled out, but SHE didn't hear.

HER ears occupied by standard issue Apple buds.

SHE just kept looking into the abyss of the dark tunnel, eager for a light to finally emerge.

I looked back to the stairs I'd just come down. If I ran, I could ascend them, clear the lobby and then descend the northbound flight in a little under thirty seconds.

I heard the sound of a train.

I heard the sound of a second.

There was no time.

"Lauren!" I yelled even louder. Everyone looked at me, everyone except HER.

The southbound train emerged from the tunnel, its blinding light growing ever closer. It was coming in at full speed, I wasn't sure if would stop or just straight up run the station.

But who knew if I would get another chance?

I stepped back to the wall, took a deep breath and then, just as the train pulled in, sprinted forward and jumped.

I don't care if I die, so long as my demise is dramatic and arguably poetic.

The silver bullet clipped the back of my jacket, but there was no pain, no harm.

I landed erratically on the other set of tracks, my foot a few inches shy of the electrified third rail.

Close call.

But then, HER train, the northbound pulled in: its massive carriage and bright lights rapidly closing in on my sprawled out body. It sounded its horn but it couldn't stop in time. Everyone looked down at me but no one acted. I remembered the usual Toronto response to a subway suicide: "Thanks for delaying my train you crazy piece of shit, why couldn't you have just hung yourself? Just cause your life sucks, why do you have to fuck up mine too?" A few of them took pictures with their phones, a few others laughed in discomfort. A few wanted to see my body torn in two as a means of breaking through the daily monotony.

I wanted to run, but I couldn't, I just froze in place.

I closed my eyes and prepared myself for the impact, hoping it would knock me out first.

I felt a great pressure on my underarms-I was being pulled up, off the tracks and to the platform.

I opened my eyes. Matt stood directly over me.

"Jesus, Sean! Are you crazy?" He screamed at me. "What the hell were you thinking!"

"Matt?" I stared at him, every inch of him, over and over again. He was forever nineteen and wearing his grey Ryerson hoodie. There was a bullet hole right between his eyes.

"Get out of here man!" He yelled at me. "Before you get yourself arrested!"

The uniforms were already responding, sprinting across the southbound platform, hands on their waists.

"Don't look back. Just go!" He yelled dramatically "and put this on!" He pulled off the hoodie and tossed it to me. As I pulled it over my chest, he turned around and I could see the back of his head. His brain and skull were fully visible through a gaping wound the size of a baseball. I pulled up the hood to conceal my face.

And then he started to fade, one pixel at a time. The resolution rapidly declined with each passing second.

"Matt...Don't go man. I need you." I pleaded desperately. And I did need him, we all did. We had always pictured him our future savoir.

"Take care of yourself, Sean." He said.

And then he was gone.

The screams of the uniforms were ringing closer.

Lauren had vanished into the crowd – an ocean of furious faces pissed off about a potential delay.

I hustled out the nearest exit and ran down Yonge Street, not looking back until I hit Bloor.

I never heard from the police.

I never saw anything about my stunt in the news.

I still had the hoodie.

Chapter Thirty-Seven

I WOKE UP TOO early. Way too early.

It was 2 am. I stood up only to fall right back onto my bed. My head weighed more than my body and the room swayed back and forth like we were on the high seas.

I threw up a thick black sludge (I'd drank plenty of Bermudian black rum the night before) all over the toilet and the bathroom floor.

My throat itched and my stomach scorched and ached. I took some Pepto, then some Advil, neither did anything to help.

On my way back to bed, I saw my phone vibrate.

There were five missed calls and a text from Nate: *Someone hurt Lindsay, what do I do?*

I chugged a couple pints of water and called him back.

"Nate?"

"Sean!" I could barely hear him-there was furious wind in the background.

"What's going on? You okay?" I asked.

"No, I'm not. Some guy roughed up Lindsay."

"What? What happened?"

"Lindsay. SHE was out with some friends at this bar in Kensington. Some guy was getting really aggressive so SHE left and then he jumped HER outside, SHE'S on HER way to the hospital."

"Christ."

"I'm going after them, Sean. I've got a gun."

"No! Nate. Listen, just come over, okay? We'll talk this out."

"No. I'm killing these guys! These motherfuckers never get what they deserve, they're going to tonight!" His speech was slurred and uncoordinated-he'd had a lot to drink.

"Nate, where are you?"

"Entering the market now."

"Nate, just get in a cab and come over, okay? Don't do anything!"

"It's too late. One of them just left Nassau. He's fucking dead!"

Nate disconnected. I called back but he didn't answer.

I went to the closet and got dressed, pausing midway to throw up again. This time, there was blood. Lots of blood.

You're dying Sean. Stop drinking. Maybe it isn't too late.

I grabbed the first cab I saw on Bloor.

"Kensington Market and step on it." I tossed a fifty onto the passenger seat and he drove like a madman.

It was 3 am and the Market was dead, completely empty, save for a homeless guy pissing in one of the alleys. I went over to Nassau, only it wasn't there, in its place there was an even nicer bar called Augusta's Lust.

I called Nate.

Number disconnected.

I tried again.

Number disconnected.

I sent him a text: *Where are you man? Are you okay?*

It was sent back-invalid number.

I went home, but I didn't sleep.

* * *

The next morning, I rented the Toyota again and drove back to Malvern, to the same cookie cutter neighborhood, only to find his house, the stale bungalow where I'd dropped him off last month entirely boarded up. The front of it was covered in general graffiti. The rooftop was on the verge of collapse: burnt to a crisp from what must have been one hell of a fire. The rest of the houses on the block were a bit decrepit, but nothing like this. It didn't belong. It was like it had been airlifted out of Detroit.

So I inquired of his neighbors, an older couple who were sitting on their front porch, smoking.

"Hey. Excuse me. What happened next door? Did the family take off?" I asked them, pointing to the house in question to minimize confusion.

"What family?"

"The Rodes. You know? Nathan? Teenage kid?"

The husband started to laugh. "Son, no one's lived at that house but squatters for years now and I've never heard of anyone named Rode."

"You sure?"

"Of course. Maybe you got the wrong address?"

I drove around the subdivision for a few minutes, but there was no question, that was his house. Wasn't it?

I dropped by his school in North York, only to have Adam stop me at the front door. He was frantic, scared to come within three feet of me as if I had the plague. "What the heck are you doing here, Sean? You know Jan says I can't see you!"

She had him on a retractable collar, no matter how far away-she could choke him with a single snap of her wrist. But I didn't care to play this game-I had bigger problems, so I just shoved him out of the way. "My God! I'm not here for you, Adam. Relax."

He came back around me and got in my way once again. "Sean, what's going on? Why are you doing this?"

"Is Nate okay? Is he at school today?" I said.

A look of perplexion "Who?"

"Nate. Nathan Rode, he's in your writer's class. Awkward kid, brilliant writer." I was speaking at a furious pace and I couldn't slow down.

"What?" he was confused, oh so confused.

"Nathan Rode!"

"Sean. I know my class list, there's no Nathan Rode in my writers craft."

"What?"

He ran his hands over his eyes, agitated. "You didn't see the doctor did you?"

I grabbed him by the collar and slammed him up against the brick wall.

"Listen I don't know what you're pulling, but

Nate's a friend of mine, okay? And I can't find him and he might be in some serious trouble, so don't mess around with me, I need to talk to him. If he's here, you better tell me, got it?"

He swallowed hard and spoke slowly and clearly. "Sean. I don't know a Nathan Rode okay? I swear to you. I wish you could hear yourself right now, you're not making any sense."

I let him go and took a step back, I thought of my mum and I started to shake.

"Sean? Are you okay?"

"I need to get out of here." I started running.

"Sean! Wait! Sean! You're sick, let me get you help! Sean!" he cried out, as I got back in the car and drove away.

And then, as I was driving, I realized. Nate's street, Ropar Drive, it wasn't in Malvern at all-it was in West Hill. It wasn't his house. It was mine.

Chapter Thirty-Eight

I WENT BACK TO the Annex apartment, not bothering to pack, though taking the necessary time to polish off the remaining bottles. After all, you can't take liquid through airport security.

"I need a flight to Los Angeles. One way." I said to the girl behind the Air Canada desk. She was gorgeous and she gave me a few hints, but I was way too scared right now to play the game.

"Certainly sir and when would you like to fly with us?"

"You have something today, LAX?"

She didn't even bother checking the computer in front of her. "I'm sorry sir, there are no planes flying today."

"What about Burbank? Ontario? Long Beach? I'll fly to any of 'em, they're all good to me. I just need to get back to Southern California, tonight. I don't care what the fare is, I'll pay anything."

"No sir, you don't understand. There's a storm moving up from The States, a very serious one in fact. All flights out of Pearson Airport are cancelled until further notice." I hadn't heard anything about a storm. Then again, I hadn't been paying attention to anything other than my novel for a long time.

"You're joking?"

"No sir. Cancelled indefinitely."

"Well what about Billy Bishop? Or Buffalo?"

"Sir, all air travel in the region has been put on hold. I'm sorry."

"Well, that's just great. When's it going to be back up?"

"I'm not sure, sir, I'm sorry. We'll be shutting down shortly, everyone will. You should get back to your hotel now while it's still clear, there's supposed to be thirty cm tonight alone. Speaking of which, if you're grounded, maybe we could?" I didn't give her an answer, I was too shaken to amuse her, let alone get it up.

I grabbed a few twelve dollar pints from the terminal's bar in an effort to call her storm bluff. Then I saw the snow start to feast on the frozen concrete, flakes the size of leaves. Turns out she was holding pocket aces. So I grabbed the express bus back Downtown and as every other passenger linked up with friends and family around Union Station, I just started walking. Destination unknown.

***

Cold, miserable nights such as these are ample opportunities to drop all obligations and just cozy up with loved ones. To find comfort and contentment in the reassuring, nonjudgmental arms of those with whom we have invested in great amounts of emotional and financial equity. We invest in these relationships each and every day – nights like these are when those investments finally pay dividends – cold, miserable Christmas Eve's, even more so.

Montreal was a long way away.

Downtown was hectic, packed to the brim with last minute shoppers and early arrivals to the 9 pm mass. As I walked along King Street I bumped into about ten packs. Each comprised of a mother, a father and their kids. None of them noticed my presence. Nor did they notice the gusts of wind, blowing fresh snow up from the street directly into their faces. They didn't notice anything. They were in a trance, completely hypnotized, their ears fixated on some carolers, their eyes, on the bright blue lights of a nearby Christmas tree, their minds on how they couldn't wait to unwrap some presents, as if what they would find underneath the wrapping paper would somehow solve the problems they faced the other 364 days of the year. Every member of the pack looked happy, wearing smiles behind their bright red cheeks. There was something magical in the air, but I wasn't breathing it.

The more of these packs I saw, the more I began to question the choices I'd made. I had three "children", my forth was due any day now, and I loved them. But they weren't here with me when it counted. They couldn't hold my hand, or hug me. I couldn't drag them to church tonight, and they wouldn't be at my bedside tomorrow morning, shaking me to get up so we could open presents together.

I had three million in the stock market, mostly

energy, and that was doing great. I also had another half a million in a savings account with Bank of America. I thought about buying something, just for the hell of it, a big gift that I could throw under a tree for tomorrow morning: maybe a Rolex? A Porsche? A bottle of Glenfiddich 50? Or maybe I could just go travel Europe, five star hotels all the way. The thought of this caused me to smile for a minute, but then sure enough, the excitement evaporated. And instead I began to wonder how much I could drink before I blacked out. I hadn't blacked out from alcohol since I was seventeen and even then, it had only been for a few minutes. That seemed strange to me, especially considering how often I heard other people refer to it. The way they spoke of it, it seemed like the "runners high" of drinking. Why did these stupid amateurs get to have all the fun?

Maybe they were just full of it? Maybe no one ever blacked out? Maybe it was just a great excuse, something you could tell your wife when she found you in bed with her sister. "Sorry, honey! I didn't even know it wasn't you! I blacked out, I swear!" A lawyer once told me that being drunk was considered a state of duress, meaning you could get out of any contract you signed if you could prove you were too intoxicated to make a rational decision. Not sure if that holds up in court, but it certainly does in personal life. "I was drunk" is an excuse we accept from others far too often.

I looked into a few of the Downtown bars, but they were too cheery, too many couples and groups of friends drinking eggnog under mistletoe, too much fun being had, not enough escapism.

So I journeyed Uptown, to Yonge and Eglinton, the trendiest palate of the stale north side, where things were far quieter. The locals here were either cooped up at home or getting festive south of Bloor. The streets were empty. I didn't bump into any packs as I made my way into a Yonge street dive bar: dark, dank, quiet, a few rats scurrying in a back corner. As soon as I sat down along the bar, I felt a warm sensation of familiarity in my stomach. I'd been here in this dump, many, many times before. I could remember a few faces I'd shared evenings with here: a blond, a brunette, an Asian girl, but no names. Even as I felt a rodent scurry over my shoe, I stayed put, I felt comfort here, a sense of belonging, as I ordered myself a supporting entourage of my tequila/bourbon concoction to lend an ear in the otherwise empty bar.

Twenty minutes later and I was already done three, another thirty minutes and I'd entirely lost count.

"Hey buddy. I'm real sorry, but you're cut off." The bartender said, capping the bottles and putting them back up on the shelf.

"What?"

"You don't look good. I'm not giving you anymore."

"Ah come on. It's Christmas Eve. Show a little holiday generosity." I pleaded.

He was a nice guy, those were rare in this town, but I could see from his simple eyes that he just didn't get it. "Look, I'll give you some water, call ya a cab, get ya home to the family, how's that? I'm sure wifey is waiting for you to get back."

"There is no wifey." I said, taking a deep breath.

"Alright, girlfriend."

"Nah." And then I missed her, Stephanie, half as much as I did Pat, and a quarter as much as I missed Lauren. Why is it? Why is it that I only start to care about them once I've lost them?

"Hooker?" he joked, giving me a pat on the back.

"That's not a half bad idea, you know anyone good?" I replied, wishing I'd taken that Air Canada girl up on her offer after all.

"I may have a card or two lying around. I'll attach one to your receipt, how's that?"

"Sounds good."

I slipped the card he gave me, a small red one with two cherries and the contact info for Lusty Layla on it, into my pocket, before making a trip to the ATM, and then, to the classier pub, right next door. The snow was already a foot high, the sidewalks and roads completely unswept, but, I was the only one making footprints.

It was a much nicer bar, but I didn't feel the same nostalgia, this place would have been well outside my student budget.

"Look, I'm here to drink, I don't want any lecture about moderation. Three hundred enough for an all you can drink? No limit?" I said to the owner sternly, I was the only customer he was likely to get tonight.

He pondered for a few seconds and then spoke "Make it five. In cash. You pass out, my guys toss you to the curb and you were never here, you understand?"

"Alright let's rock."

"Merry Christmas Pal." I felt better being in a bar with an asshole tender. He would be as anxious to kill me as I was.

A lot of people think the key to getting smashed is to drink fast. It's not. Sure, chugging can have its benefits, especially when you're in a rush. But when you want a real, lasting high without the threat of regurgitation, the credo really is, slow and steady wins the race. The higher the percentage the better. Only frat boys and amateurs choose beer or bar rails. For me, it's all about that 151.

Shot glasses can be a good way for beginners to gage their levels and through visual assistance, keep their intake below their plateau. I, on the other hand prefer my spirits in a glass. I don't require an abacus to know my limit. Plus at this percentage an ounce can be too much at a time. But a delicate sip, each and every ninety seconds is as tolerable as it is potent. Even at this snail's pace, you'd be amazed how quickly you can get to the bottom.

Everyone experiences their peak differently, some people become the life of the party, others become brash, violent savages, while others burst into tears. Me, I find myself at the centre of a mime's box, a hypnotist's punch line. The rest of the world ceases to exist.

So when SHE came in, shaking HER head playfully to clear the clumps of snow from HER hair before removing HER drenched P-Coat, shutting down HER brand new Blackberry Pearl and ordering a glass of wine, taking a seat two stools down from me, I found myself unable to react. I was unable to speak, unable to budge. So I just sat there, watching HER right in front of me, on TV in 4D.

"Here ya go, miss." The bartender glided into the scene, carrying HER drink."Thank you." SHE smiled and began to sip it sensually.

"I don't mean to pry, but I can't help but wonder. What's a pretty girl like you, doing in a place like this on Christmas Eve? Tell me you have someone to go home too." The tender said, in a fatherly tone.

"You don't have to worry about me. I'm just killing some time, meeting up with someone soon, Downtown." SHE replied, taking a large sip.

"Oh ya?

"Yeah." SHE grinned.

"I hope you don't mind me saying. He's a damn lucky guy."

"He sure is" SHE replied, with a giggle, gently stroking HER necklace-an emerald on a gold chain.

I like to think that when I'm out in public I generally exhibit good drinking etiquette. Though, every once in a while we all just get the urge. So, as a nightcap, I ordered six ounces of whiskey in a pint glass and dropped it in one, violent session. It put me in a conscious purgatory, robbed of my senses, as I teetered the fine line between ecstasy and nausea. Oh My God. I'm gonna die.

When I came back down SHE was gone. In HER place was a folded cocktail napkin.

Sean, Meet you at On The Rocks, The Distillery,

tonight, midnight. Don't keep me waiting... I Love You. Lauren. XoXo.

The snow was so bad that the TTC was suspended, so there was no subway or bus service to get me to The Distillery. So I walked, knee high, down Yonge Street, fueled by this tingling in my stomach. The same tingling I'd felt the first time I'd ever put my arm around a girl in a movie theater.

A youthful, wishful state of utter stupidity.

It was the greatest feeling in the world.

CHAPTER THIRTY-NINE

The Distillery.

I T WAS TORONTO'S historic district.
It used to be where whiskey and beer were produced.

Now, it was a yuppie haven: filled with fine restaurants, edgy art galleries, chic condos and upscale bars.

Along its crude stone streets, an eerie instrumental rang out from invisible speakers, a seasonal hymn drained of its ability to comfort by sheer repetition. Along the dark narrow alleys, where I expected to see festive yuppie families exiting the restaurants after turkey dinners, I found only shadows, sans a source. At the center of it all, a wire bound Christmas Tree – its undercarriage entirely bare.

It was Christmas Eve and yet, the only place in the area with any element of cheer to it was a nightclub on the southern edge of The Distillery called On the Rocks. It was a brand new five story building, painted entirely black, celebrating its grand opening on a night where no sane person would ever want to be out clubbing. I realized then that this was the first Christmas I'd be spending alone.

There was a long line. It was filled with homogenous manikins who served no purpose greater than that of place-holders. One bragged on and on for agonizing minutes about how they'd seen in the corner of their eye, a washed up C-lister in Yorkville the night before, as if it even mattered.

So thirsty…

Fifty dollars later I was out of the cold and into the bar. Where blistering heat managed to distract nearly as much as the flashing vivid lights, rotating between four different shades of red, while retro music from the previous decade radiated out of the stereo system. The place wasn't overly large but it was packed to its capacity, a few hundred suits and dresses two stepping off beat in the normal Toronto fashion. I pushed my way through the sweaty crowd and over to the central bar, where a single tender frantically worked to address fifty orders. I waited in queue, until I finally got his attention.

"Scotch, please." Neat."

He looked at me and smirked. "You sure? I got a double tequila, double bourbon for you, if you want it. On the house."

"Really? Why?" I figured maybe the owner had recognized me and was excited to have a celebrity at his opening.

"Yeah, from that lovely lady over there." He began to survey the crowd. "I've never seen a guy get a drink bought for him and I've been tending in Toronto for twenty years. Lock her down, that one's a keeper. Ah there she is!"

I followed his long index finger and caught a good look at HER. SHE was dressed in a long black cocktail dress, HER hair flowing dramatically in the stale air, holding a martini glass with one hand, signaling me seductively with the other. SHE was asking me to follow HER into the VIP section, a small room at the back, separated from the rest of the bar by a red curtain. A bouncer stood in front of it, two looks and I realized it was the same bouncer from Nassau.

I anxiously waited for the tender to finish pouring the drink then I kicked it in a single swig and chased after HER, pushing through a mob of dancing fools, ignorant to my existence. Ignorant to anything and everything but their own cheap gratification.

SHE blew me an overblown kiss in slow motion as SHE walked through the velvet, the curtains swaying behind HER before immediately restoring themselves to calm. The bouncer looked at me, nodded and then stepped out of the way. "Go ahead sir. You've been added to the list." What list?

This was it. I hesitated for a second in indecision, trying to figure out what I would say, what I would do, entirely unsure of either, when I heard HER shout out to me.

"Sean, come on!"

Okay, it's time. I held my breath, excitement to a boil within my nauseous stomach.

But when I stepped through the curtains, SHE was gone.

It wasn't a VIP section. In fact, there was nothing in

the empty storage room save for one seemingly foreign object. A noose, tied crudely out of a computer's patch cord, attached to a cold steel pipe, swinging rhythmically from side to side.

The music, which had been pumping with a furious energy stopped, the murmurs of the drunken idiots too.

I stood in silence while I watched it, waving, like a pendulum, back and forth, back and forth, never losing momentum, despite the fact that there was nothing to keep it going. I turned back towards the curtains seeking an exit, but finding in their place, a solid concrete wall. There was no exit, no escape, and so, I just stood there and watched it swing, back and forth, back and forth.

And then, just like that, there was no more brain fog, no more confusion, just like that, I remembered everything.

* * *

I'm twenty-two. I'm back in that tiny apartment in Hollywood, sitting on the floor, chugging a tall can. It's only my fifth week in town, I haven't met Hanson yet.

Beside me, my phone is vibrating, there are six new texts. One from my mum, one from Adam, one from Patty, and three from HER. Back then, I got texts every day, but I never answered them, or the calls. What was I gonna say? That my new life sucked? That everything I had ever promised them had been nothing more than childish fantasy? That I was a failure?

I open the first message from Lauren:

Sean, please, please, please call me. You have no idea how badly I need you right now. Lauren.

Then the second:

Sean, please, please, call me. You are the only one who can help me. Lauren.

And then the third.

Sean...I'm sorry...I can't...Goodbye...

* * *

I'm back in the Distillery, right in front of where I thought On the Rocks was. Only, it's not a nightclub now, it's a condo.

And then I longed for the ignorance once more. I had been such a fool to take it for granted.

CHAPTER FORTY

I WALKED NORTH FROM the Distillery, shivering in the bitter, relentless cold. It was at least minus twenty, maybe minus forty with the wind-chill. The everlasting snow fall exacerbated that further, it was up to my waist now. But I kept walking, up to Moss Park where, exhausted, I took a seat on a four foot high pile of snow against a tall oak tree, next to a bum drinking rye from a paper bag. He had a hat on, gloves too, along with a Toronto Argos jacket, but they were all cheap, thin, so he was trembling uncontrollably. When he saw me, he forced his body still.

"Hey buddy, could you spare a shot?" I asked him.

He clinched it tightly to his chest. "Fuck you, man, this is mine."

I tossed over my wallet. "You can have it?"

"Sure." He snatched the wallet in a heartbeat and then passed the bottle over. I took a generous swig while he opened it with the excitement of a kid on their birthday.

"Wow! There's a lot in here, man!"

"Yeah well, Merry Christmas."

"Thanks buddy! God bless!" He said through chattering teeth.

"You know? There's enough in there, you could take yourself to a motel tonight, get yourself out of this cold."

"Yeah. Maybe." He replied, disinterested.

"Hell, there's enough in there that after that you could buy yourself some decent food, a razor, some new clothes."

"Yeah. Maybe."

"But hey, you could do that even without the money, couldn't you? You could get yourself to a shelter – there are a ton of them nearby." I pointed to the nearest one, a two minute walk, if that. "They could put you up for the winter. Get you some good food, some health care, some medication. Hell I even hear they do job training and work placement in those things."

He paused for a second in thought. "Yeah. Or there's enough in this wallet for me to just get really, really, really, fucking wasted."

I took another sip and felt a bit warmer. "Yeah, that's also true."

"Cause look, man. I don't need some shelter. I've been on the streets ten years. I'll be here at least ten more. I'm an ex-Arctic Marine – I can take this no problem. I don't need some shithole shelter and all their preaching and whining, like any of the jackasses there even know what they're talking about. All I need to stay warm is a few ounces. " He had his legs and arms pressed firmly into his torso, doing everything in his power to sit still.

A gust of wind hit my face, searing it, before my

cheeks went completely numb. The only part of my body with any feeling left was my right hand which clinched onto the bottle. "Well, I guess that's your call."

"Damn straight."

I took another small sip. "So, tell me something man, you believe in hell?"

"Hell? Sure. Look all around you." He pointed, out to a sea of likeminded individuals, cradling themselves to no avail, armed with nothing more than ragged blankets and torn twenty year old ski jackets in the subzero conditions. "All these good people, at least a third will be frozen by New Years, while they spent all the taxes on subways to nowhere. This city is hell."

"I mean the afterlife Hell."

"Sure. Look forward to it-at least it's nice and warm down there. No more Canadian winters."

"Yeah, well I'll see you there."

"Cheers to that brother." He took the bottle back and had another sip. "A toast then."

Out of nowhere, my stomach began to ache, worse than it ever had before. It hurt so bad that I could no longer sit upright, so I bent over and clenched it tightly, begging a being greater than I to let it stop.

"Hey, buddy. You okay?" The bum asked.

I was no longer cold, the bum kept talking but I didn't hear him. The only thing I could think about was the sting and how I'd throw myself in front of a subway if I couldn't get it to stop.

Then the ache turned to a vicious itch. I began scratching my stomach but it did nothing to relieve the discomfort. Then the itch turned to a burn, I put my hand on my stomach and it was an oven.

"I'm fine." I said between harsh coughs, each one produced some blood and I wiped my hands clean in the snow.

He handed the bottle back to me. "Have another drink, you'll feel better."

I took it from him and threw it against the nearest tree, it smashed on impact, ten ounces lost in the fresh powder. It was the first time I had ever wasted a drop.

He grabbed my shoulder and shook me "Hey man! That was mine!"

The burning intensified, I needed to get home.

I got up from the mount. "There's plenty in my wallet, buy yourself a whole case, or better yet, get yourself to a shelter or a hotel. You don't have to be one of the third." I said to him.

"You asshole! The stores are all closed till Boxing Day! What am I gonna do now!" He screamed back.

I went home to The Annex to take a cold shower. When I took off my shirt I could see my entire stomach had gone a shade of light red. That and my teeth were stained pink.

I spent the rest of the night drinking water by the pint to try and stop the room from spinning. I told myself I'd never drink again.

I don't believe you anymore.

I don't either…

And, the bum, wallet with five hundred dollars in hand, a hundred feet from a shelter with advertised vacancy or a five minute walk from two hotels, chose to stay put.

He froze to death by morning.

Chapter Forty-One

I PICKED UP A paper with my Advil at the corner store. I wanted to read the most recent literary reviews.

While flipping through the pages, I saw a story that made my heart stop.

The headline read: *Toronto woman, twenty-eight, mother of two, viciously beaten and left for dead in the Kennedy subway station by her own husband.*

There was a photo of her, before and after, it was Patty.

It was tenth page news, demoted in importance by a five year international study which suggested that caffeine may not be ideal for toddlers, a celebrity being kicked out of a Yorkville restaurant for shooting heroin right at her table and the front page announcement that a new NHL team may be coming to North York by 2021.

The whole thing had been captured on the TTC cameras. It had started off a simple argument on the empty westbound platform, but it quickly escalated. Screaming turned to spiting, which turned to shoving, then to striking, then she was unconscious and he was overtop of her, smashing her head into the floor a dozen times. She had survived the ordeal, but there was a serious risk of brain injury.

Alan was a forty-nine year old former CA who had been let go five years back on account of his drinking. Since then his rap sheet had come to feature assault, extortion and five DUI charges. He had vanished and police were desperate for tips.

I knew I could find him. I thought about informing the police, but decided not to.

I'd played this game before-he wasn't going to do serious time. Five years at most, then he'd come back more vicious than ever. He had to be taken out of the picture. The skull or the liver, something had to give.

I found Patty's address on Victoria Park Avenue and mapped a five km radius around it. And then I started scouting the bars, the very worst ones, the ones where people knew to keep their mouths shut. There were five I figured were his type. I went back to each of them every night for the next three days. Manhunt or not, he was going to get thirsty. He couldn't go to the liquor stores, they all had cameras.

I finally caught sight of him, on the third night, at the fifth and final bar on my crawl. It was a local joint around Danforth and Main, full of a male only forty plus crowd. They sat along the bar watching hockey, drinking cheap watered down whiskey, consuming cigarettes by the pack, even though there was a city wide ban on smoking inside. One guy ranted about how the war in the Middle East had gone perfectly and that he was really happy we'd taken our share of oil from the "sand niggers". Another claimed the solution to the "emerging gay problem" was to force all young men to do ten years military service out of high school. Another said everyone living on the street should be lined up and shot.

It was a spot the west side hipsters snickered about but wouldn't dare venture to for fear of getting their scrawny necks broken. The bartender was a fat old woman covered in tattoos.

Alan was sitting in the center of the bar drinking an English cider, ten empty glasses lay in front of him-he'd been there all night.

Anyone could tell, he had once been a looker. But the charisma had long since been washed away by the crashing, blistering waves of beer and bourbon. Now he was a good eighty pounds overweight and bordering on a triple chin, his hair was almost all gone and his teeth were turning yellow. He let out a loud belch, hacking up a bit of vomit in the process.

"Hey man, you mind if I sit with you?" I asked him, pointing to the adjacent empty stool.

"Free county, last time I checked." He replied, his speech slurred by a liquor lisp.

"Thanks." I sat down and ordered two shots of rye. "One for me, and one for my new friend."

"Thanks pal." He spit when he talked, some of the residue made it onto my face.

"It's my pleasure. I had a good day today, got myself a nice little bonus from the suits upstairs. And happiness loves company. Am I right?" I gave him a friendly pat on the back.

"Cheers to that partner." We clanged glasses as I

restrained the urge to tear his pudgy head off right then and there.

"Haven't seen you around here before. You new to the east side?" He inquired.

"Yeah. Just moved here from Los Angeles."

"Oh yea? That dump? I came here from Oakville. You know it?" A rich suburb to the west.

"Sure."

"Left that paradise behind, all for some stupid bitch. Amazing the decisions we make when drunk and hard, Christ."

"Oh, you sound married?"

"Four years and counting. Got two little shits too." He had taken his ring off and was twirling it on the counter, it was covered in grime.

"Bummer."

"You got that straight. Should'a used a rubber, brother. Take some advice, fuck all you want, but don't ever let them lock you down with that pregnancy bullshit. Selfish bitch, should have used a coat hanger like I told her, then I never would have had to put my dick in a retirement home! Christ I should'a pushed the cunt down the stairs when I had the chance." I laughed at the ludicrousness of his mentality as much as the very cliché of it. He was just another "bad boy" grown too old to make it look charming. The world was filled to the brim with them.

I found myself clenching my fist, so hard it was beginning to turn red. "You know? You remind me of someone." I said to him.

"That a fact? Who?"

"Another round!" I requested of the bartender as

she passed by. "Mix each drink with two shots tequila, two shots bourbon, will ya?"

Alan put his arm around me and pulled me in close with drunken affection. "Fucker drinks like a real man! You're alright you know that! This one's on me sailor."

"Nah, don't worry about it. Put it all on my tab." I countered. I had a wallet stacked with hundred dollar bills.

"Won't say no to that. But the way I put 'em down, you might just live to regret it." Alan chirped.

"Try me." I'd only had four pints today, he didn't stand a chance.

The bell rang and the heavyweight bout began. I didn't just maintain his pace-I grossly exceeded it, hit for hit, for the full twelve rounds of throw down with an unanimous decision. It was forty-eight ounces of 40 percent and that was simply insane. I should have been dead, but I didn't even feel sick.

"Christ, I gotta get home, get some of that snatch before I black the fuck out." He groaned, propping himself up, only to fall flat on his ass a second later. "Ah! Even gravity is out to get me tonight!" I looked into his eyes and saw them jetting in every direction, sweat poured down his forehead, his hands kept shaking, his body had reached its boiling point.

"Yeah, I should head out too. Split a cab?" I said.

"Sure. I don't know how I'd get home anyway."

"I'll help you."

I lifted him to his feet, put an arm around him, dropped a few hundreds onto the bar and led him outside and up a nearby alley. It was 2 am and a cold night-there was silence in the air. I led him far enough that I could no longer make out the cars on the Danforth.

"Hey buddy, I gotta piss like a pregnant bitch, hold up." He joked.

As soon as his pudgy fingers took hold of the zipper I laid him down with a blow to the back of his hairy neck. Then I struck him again, a hook punch to his temple.

While he rolled around on the ground in desperation, I reached into my back pocket and pulled out a bottle of cheap rubbing alcohol I'd bought at the pharmacy earlier that evening.

"What the fuck, man?!" he pulled himself back up to his knees-a kick to his flustered face prevented further counteraction.

"You're a good drinker, you know that? One of the best I've ever seen outside my family. So I've got something new for you to try. We used to hit this down in Mexico, back when I was a kid."

"You son of a bitch!"

I hit him again, this time in his obese throat and while he choked uncontrollably for air-I pressed his head back, pinched his nose to keep his mouth open and poured the poison down his gullet.

"There we go! That's a good boy. Take it back!"

He made gesture to regurgitate, though gravity made for a trusty ally, as the half pint of 97.5 percent made its way southbound into his ulcer ridden stomach.

"Come on – don't fight it-just give in. Buzz of your lifetime, I promise." I held his head back for a full minute after – to give it all time to sink in-then I threw him harshly to the ground.

In our society, the only time it's socially acceptable for a man to cry is while he is irresponsibly intoxicated, and he did, wept like a newborn, while he puked up the clear fluid. His entire body trembled-his skin adopted hues of bluish grey.

He grabbed hold of my pant leg and begged. "Help me man! Please! Help me! I'm so sick! Get me to a hospital!"

"Get off me!" I pushed him back down to the puke covered concrete where he kept hacking, more clear fluid and then some blood.

I looked away to make sure no one was watching.

When I looked back at his face, it was gone and in its place I saw my father's. His stone cold eyes looking me over as he cracked a grin.

I took a step back and froze in place.

I knew that if he came at me I was done for. I wouldn't be able to hit back, I'd just stand there as he beat me to death, one blow from his iron knuckles after another. I was a grown man, but staring there at my dad I was a helpless thirteen year old.

"Think you're tough enough, Sean? Take your best fucking shot." He said, stretching his arms out to maximize the target. "Go on, try me!"

A shadow with no body behind it cruised over his frame.

And then the man in front of me was just plain old Alan.

I regained my composure.

I hit him again, in the knee, hard enough to shatter it. I didn't want him trying to get up again.

I'm told it's the most painful injury you can endure, but he didn't seem to notice-he was completely focused on the vicious coughs as his stomach shook abnormally with each and every gasp.

I let him suffer for a few minutes.

When I got bored of that, I rolled him onto his back and pressed my shoe into his stomach. He began to choke.

I looked up at the brick wall of an apartment building. On it, a projector reel began to roll. I saw Patty and then I saw my Mother. First, as beautiful young things with endless potential and then as broken souls aged well beyond their years by the torrents of abuse.

The liver or the skull…

I kneeled down in front of him and started striking his face, over and over again, not stopping until I had broken both my hands.

When I stood back up, I couldn't make out where his head ended and the concrete began.

I expected to feel guilt, or remorse, or at the very least, fear. But, instead, I felt only immense gratification at Alan's expiry. I looked down and realized I was hard.

As I was walked out of the alley I caught my reflection in a window: my father looked back at me and winked.

CHAPTER FORTY-TWO

IT'S A SUNNY summer day. I'm eighteen.

SHE wants to check out a carnival down by the lake.

HER older brother Dave drives us there. He's always hated me, but SHE convinces him to play nice.

SHE tells me SHE wants to win one of those gigantic teddy bears, we'll be further apart come September and SHE needs something to cuddle up with in HER York University dorm.

I know all the games in the midway are rigged but I promise HER I'll win HER one anyhow. I try the ring toss, the trick shooting and then attempt to knock over some glass milk bottles with a flimsy plastic ball. It does not go well.

SHE goes to find some cotton candy and I slip the carnie a fifty. It means I'll be eating canned food for a week but when I see how happy SHE is with the giant blue bear, my stomach cuts me some slack.

SHE tells me SHE's cold and I give HER my hoodie, Matt's Ryerson hoodie.

My mum always told me the rides at these things

were death traps operated by strung out crackheads. But when SHE asks me to go on the Ferris wheel – I say yes without hesitation.

At the top you can see the whole skyline and it's gorgeous, but my eyes are locked on HER. Since we've met, the environment has become largely trivialized.

SHE grips my hand, and I kiss HER. The whole world stops. Nothing else matters. Not my dad, not my student debt, not the thirst. In this moment, everything is, as it should be. I tell HER I love HER, for the first time. SHE says it back. SHE makes me promise I'll always be there. I tell HER I will. In this moment, the gaping void in my stomach finds itself corked. And I become completely content with the horrors of this sociopathic world.

In the back of my mind I tell myself that if I ever lose HER I'll kill myself.

* * *

It's a cold December night. I'm twenty-seven.

I'm sitting in an empty parking lot in the west side, drinking rye from a paper bag. The carnival had once been held here annually. Now, it's the pre-construction site of some million dollar condos.

My father is sitting there beside me, drinking from his own paper bag. I nod to him and we clang bottles.

"You get it now, don't you?" He says to me.

I nod.

"None of us want to be this way."

"I know." I say.

"You're a lot like me, Sean."

No, I'm not.

Yes you are.

"For what it's worth, it wasn't your fault." He says. "You had to leave. Just like I had to leave Dublin."

It wasn't worth it, now was it?

Not at all.

"I should have been there for HER. For Mum. For everyone." I say.

"I should have been there for you." He replies. "None of us know what the fuck we're doing, none of us know the rules to the game until it's already been lost."

I start to cry, weep, as I fondle the note SHE left for me before SHE did it. It's really quite a brilliant poem-could have been published.

He reaches over and we embrace. I rest my head in his shoulder and for the first time in my life I feel an actual connection with him. "I love you, Sean." He says.

"I love you too, Dad."

"I'll be seeing you real soon." He says. "I've got a flask there waiting for ya."

He fades away and I'm left there alone, sitting right underneath where the Ferris wheel had once been. There's a construction crane in its place.

There is no amount of money that can stop the world now.

* * *

I go to Mount Pleasant, where I visit all three graves. Beside HER's I dig a small hole, where I bury the Fifth Avenue engagement ring.

Ten Feet Down – it had always just seemed like a

cool title, I'd never given much thought to its greater meaning.

When hanging one's self, ten feet is the height you need to drop to break your neck.

PART VIII

2013

Los Angeles, California.

CHAPTER FORTY-THREE

I'M BACK IN L.A. now, confined twenty-three hours a day within a spacious two million dollar two bedroom along Ocean Ave, in the heart of Santa Monica, but a block from the beach. After dark, the dealers and their junkies do business out on the sand, I watch them from the safety of my tenth story balcony and I don't care, I'm way too high up to ever get hit by a stray. I finally get it now.

The hour I'm out, fifty minutes are spent in my BMW 7 Series, the doors always locked, the windows always rolled up, even on sunny days. I don't look out them anymore. The only thing I ever see anywhere in this city is my own reflection.

The books done. It's an international bestseller. Hanson is richer and his trophy wife blows him more frequently. I'm more successful, more acclaimed, in the running for a Pulitzer. Chances are, I'll be remembered.

The fridge is fully stocked – keeping it that way is my number one priority. The bottles, of Polish vodka, Canadian rye, Irish whiskey and Mexican tequila accumulate in the dozens monthly, the beer cans by the hundreds. The neighbors keep their mouth shut, not to be polite, but rather they genuinely don't care, the only ones in this city who do, are the bottlers, who make their rounds every morning. They consider me their savior. One even wrote me a letter saying I had single handedly got him off the street. If I up my consumption maybe I can start my own charity.

I've had a few new girlfriends but things haven't worked out. I care for each new one about half as much as the previous. Hanson assures me this is normal, that the diminishing returns eventually drive all men to prostitutes. I tried one but couldn't get myself into it, every time she checked her watch, I lost my erection.

I'll never be in love again. I'll never be loved again. Most everyone comes to this bitter realization. Most aren't twenty-seven when they do.

But, whatever, that's just fine, because the liquor is there for me, through thick and thin, its protection and emotional support as dependable as the ripping, roaring tide a hundred or so feet from my doorstep.

My stomach hurts a lot more these days, the night of and the morning after. So much so that once the painkillers wear off I have to grit my teeth to keep from screaming. But I haven't seen a doctor, nor do I plan too, he would just tell me to stop drinking and that is simply not an option.

The way I see it, it's just the toll to pay in order to ride, you drop in the coins like you would on the city bus, sit down and hope it takes you somewhere worthwhile. Even if it is the same route, over and over and over again you just keep hoping that one day the route will be extended and you'll find yourself somewhere new, somewhere worthwhile.

It's an inevitability-a one-to-one sure bet. Just as Los Angeles will eventually be eradicated from this continent via earthquake, I too am destined for an early, violent demise. These paths are chosen for us, all of us, and played out through our own consistent, unbreakable chains of action.

Despite all the breakthroughs we've made, the earth is still flat.

And no matter how well we navigate the turbulent seas with improvised compasses, in search of riches and undiscovered lands, we will all eventually reach the unforgiving edge where, while teetering, we will be forced to face our flaws, our failures, our faults.

My name is Sean Cyril O'Connor and I am an Alcoholic...

CHAPTER FORTY-FOUR

The Los Angeles Globe, April 2, 2013

Author Sean O'Connor found dead in home
By Michael Ortis

Acclaimed author Sean O'Connor has died at age twenty-nine. O'Connor died Wednesday in his Santa Monica condominium, Justin Lopez, Chief Investigator for the Los Angeles county coroner has informed The Globe.

The cause of death has been determined to be drug related. "Toxicology reports found traces of Amobartibal, an illegal barbiturate derivative once used as a sleeping aid, in his system" reveals Lopez. "We also found a great deal of alcohol. We believe the two having been used together proved fatal." However, Lopez does not believe this to be a suicide. "The quantity of Amobartibal was not particularly high-we believe O'Connor simply intended to put himself to sleep-only he never woke up."

O'Connor first found success with his controversial debut novel *Dead Heart*, published when he was only twenty-three. He quickly followed up on it with his equally impactful works: *Old Money* and *Anything for a Dollar* which cemented his reputation as one of the top young talents in the industry. Just recently, his long awaited forth novel, *Ten Feet Down* was released to critical and commercial acclaim, resulting in the young Canadian author being awarded a Pulitzer Prize for fiction.

None of O'Connor's friends or family were available for comment but Mark Hanson, O'Connor's manager, had this to say: "It's a real tragedy, Sean was a fantastic writer who had accomplished so much at such a young age, the writing community will miss him immensely." When asked if he believed the death to be a suicide he replied. "The pills? Nah, it was an accident. But Sean had been in a really dark place for a really long time. I only wish he could have seen himself the way I saw him. The way all those who admired him saw him. But they never do..."

www.ingramcontent.com/pod-product-compliance
Lightning Source LLC
Chambersburg PA
CBHW051418170626
46809CB00006B/2225